FLIGHT OF THE FALCON

Carol Kerry-Green

* * *

Flight of the Falcon

Edited by C L Jennison Editorial
Cover by: Mayflower Studio

For my husband Steve

Chapter One

Hugh

"So?" Imogen Lovell turned away from the window with its view of the Minster and focused her attention on Hugh. "What do you think? Is he the one?"

"I don't know yet," Hugh replied. He moved over to take her spot at the window and looked through the scope they had set up there overlooking Stonegate Alley.

"Bit early to tell?" Imogen continued moving around the living room, collecting her scarf and laptop bag as she did so. "Well, I'll leave you to get on with it. I have a train to catch."

Hugh looked up again. There was nothing much happening in the alley; tourists were moving from shop to shop looking for books or gifts depending on what took their fancy.

There'd been no sight of Falcon Byrde, his quarry who owned the bookshop. He shook his hands out and stretched to the ceiling. He hated surveillance jobs, but if his boss was right and Byrde *had* been involved in the bombing of the Goodkind family…

"I'll walk with you to the station," he told Imogen, his best friend and substitute sister. "I need to stretch my legs and get some groceries, I'm sure there's a Tesco or Sainsburys around here somewhere."

Imogen nodded. Her blonde hair was caught up in a tidy chignon and she had dressed with care in a Donna Karan business suit, which suited her slim body. Not that it did anything for Hugh. He enjoyed women as friends, but his interests lay elsewhere.

As they let themselves out of the rented maisonette above several of the shops on Davygate, he was surprised again at the number of tourists out and about. He knew York was a busy tourist spot, but the sheer numbers were more than he'd expected. Sidestepping a group of Japanese sightseers, he was glad the roads were closed to traffic down here, otherwise there could have been an accident.

He steered Imogen around the bulk of the tourists, the early May spring weather had brought them all out. Imogen gave him a look and he grimaced. He knew she was quite capable of looking after herself but the years of being a bodyguard before he joined his current agency wouldn't allow him to put anyone he was walking with in the way of danger.

Hugh listened to Imogen's casual conversation as they walked over Lendal Bridge, heading toward the railway station. He took note of the old walls surrounding the city, which he'd have to make time to walk along. Hugh was a big history buff, which had contributed towards him taking this job. He replied to Imogen where necessary, but his attention was elsewhere, watching the crowds, assessing everything. He made a mental note to check how high the River Ouse could flood as it looked high when they passed. Would it reach as far as Stonegate? He didn't think so, but his mind couldn't help exploring various possibilities.

"Hmm, sorry?" He realised they'd arrived at the station and that Imogen had addressed him again.

"I said I'd call you when I got back to the office. Really, Hugh, it's not like you to walk around with your head in the clouds."

"Sorry, just lots to think on here. Check with Peter when he's going to get me the final files on the Byrde brothers sent over. Anything he can find could prove useful."

"I'll mention it. You have everything you need?" she asked, referring to the equipment he'd requested.

"For now, I'll text or email you if I need anything else."

"I'll be off then, my train is nearly here." With that, she leaned in and kissed his cheek, and with a casual wave, she merged into the crowd heading for the platform and her train to Manchester.

Hugh watched her until she was out of sight, before turning to leave the station once more. As he walked, he began thinking about his current assignment. Right from the beginning, when his boss Robert Swales had called him into his office, something had seemed off. He headed back the way he'd come, stopping in at a local supermarket on the way. Though he couldn't pinpoint it any further than that. He had no idea how long he would be in York, so made sure to stock up with basics for at least a week. He'd probably eat out for part of it, but if it became necessary and he needed to stay in place for awhile, he'd need easy meals he could grab quickly.

He let himself into the maisonette and made his way to the main living area. Nothing seemed to have changed from when he had looked through the scope earlier. He could see that most of the shops were doing a brisk trade, and he catalogued them mentally once more.

Falcon Books was owned and run by Falcon Byrde, the eldest of the Byrde brothers and the focus of the current investigation. Next there was *Phoenix Antiques,* run by the middle brother known to all as Nix. Across from them was the *Wool Emporium,* run by youngest brother Robin. *Piper's Coffee Shop* was next door to that. The owner was known as Pip, who was next in age to Falcon. *Everything Crystal* was owned and run by Ollie, and last was Raven who owned *Cameo* a high-quality jewellers.

Six brothers and six shops, all set in a courtyard which had once been part of a larger shopping complex. It had been in use until the early 2010s when most of it had been sold off and converted to apartments. Apart from the six units below, which had originally been twelve but had since been converted to larger shops with accommodation. Hugh had read the initial reports on the brothers and their businesses when he'd been assigned to this job. Now he could look down and see how the conversions had been carried out.

As there was still no sign of his quarry, he decided it would be okay to go down and take a stroll amongst the shops. He could do with a coffee and though he could make one here, he could do some reconnaissance downstairs.

#

Hugh wandered around the courtyard ostensibly window shopping, but he was on high alert. Though he hadn't seen Falcon Byrde through the scope, that didn't mean he wasn't there. He could be in his flat above the shop or in a back room.

The bookshop window had a display on local history and he read the titles with interest, noting one book he'd like to purchase if he could get them to take it from the window.

Entering, he smiled at the young woman who was behind the till in the main part of the shop.

"Welcome to Falcon Books!" she chirped, almost bouncing on her feet. She looked very young and Hugh put her age at 17, 18 at most.

"Feel free to wander around," she continued. "Each section has a card telling you what's there so you can find what you're looking for. Fiction is at the front and non-fiction is at the back of the shop. There's a good mixture of old and new. Call out if you can't find anything."

"Thanks, I'll let you know." He decided to leave the book in the window for the moment and investigate further.

He bypassed the fiction and headed straight for the non-fiction and the history section, all the while looking and assessing. At some point, maybe today, he would need to plant some small cameras and listening devices in the shop. This visit would give him the opportunity to scope out good places to conceal them.

After about fifteen minutes of perusing the shelves, he'd already managed to get one small camera hidden. He'd tucked it away in an upright part of the wooden shelving. It was pretty well disguised and pointed right towards the door. He'd have to come back a couple of times to get a full complement in. Often in situations like this, he would break in overnight and plant his devices, but with the owner living above the shop, he didn't think that would be possible.

Picking up a copy of the same book he'd seen in the window, he took it to the teenager on the till.

"Great choice!" She grinned at him. "Thanks. Is the café here any good?"

"Definitely!" Her enthusiasm for everything could grate

after a while, but he smiled back. "Just tell them Abbie sent you and they'll look after you."

Hugh thanked her again and picking up his book, headed out to the café.

#

Falcon

"Watch your step." Falcon Byrde turned to his younger brother Robin and shone his torch on the slippery steps they were currently navigating.

Robin just grunted and negotiated them with no problem. Falcon watched for a few moments to make sure he was back on stable-ish ground before moving off again. Robin got around on a pair of prosthesis, having lost both his legs in a childhood medical experiment gone wrong. Falcon, the oldest of the siblings, had always felt responsible for his younger brothers, but especially Robin.

"I'm okay, Fal." Robin interrupted his thoughts then. "This is child's play compared to some of the exercises Francis put us through."

Falcon smiled as he thought of their protector and saviour. When Francis Byrde, an eccentric philanthropist, had heard about the children being used for drug experiments, he'd mounted a rescue and saved them all. He hadn't stopped there, though. No, Francis had adopted them all, giving them his last name and the prestige that came with it. Fal, Robin and their siblings had been very lucky.

His attention brought back to the present, Falcon looked around the rough passage, they'd entered through an old drainage system and were now well below York Minster.

The walls had been roughly hewn out of the bedrock and it was barely high enough for Robin to walk through. Falcon, who was a good five inches taller than his brother, was having to stoop. "It certainly feels old," Robin said as he shone his torch around, brightening the gloom.

"How did Father McKenzie say he'd found it again?"

"When he was a younger man, he was tasked with tracing some of the tunnels they found when they excavated the Minster in the 60s."

"I thought all that was on display in the undercroft?" Robin asked.

"What they want the public to see is, yes. It seems there were tunnels running close to where the Roman basilica had been. This is what he had been tasked with investigating."

"So why come to you now?"

Falcon paused, thinking about his meeting withe Father McKenzie the day before…

#

"Fal?" Abbie had shouted for him from the till.

"What?" he asked as he came into the main room of the bookshop, carrying books to be shelved.

"This gentleman says he'd like a word with you." She grinned at him as she gestured to the older man standing at her side. He was dressed in a black cassock with a white clerical collar around his neck. He smiled slightly.

Falcon held his hand out. "Falcon Byrde, how may I help you?"

"It's a pleasure to meet you, Mr Byrde. Francis sings your praises all the time." "You know my father?"

"Oh, yes, we've known each other since we were at school

together."

Falcon smiled. His father knew many people. If this man had been at school with him, he was either older than he appeared or Francis had been on one of his investigations.

"Pleased to meet you. What can I help you with?" he repeated.

"It might be best if we went somewhere a bit more private," the older man replied, indicating Abbie with his eyes. She was watching both men avidly as though they were there purely for her entertainment.

"Yes, forgive me. Let's go to my study." Hugh turned to his assistant. "We'll be in my study, Abbie, and not to be disturbed. Unless it's one of my brothers, or Francis."

Abbie nodded and turned away to serve a customer. *That girl is as curious as she is hyper,* Falcon thought as he led the older man to his study.

"I'm sorry, I didn't introduce myself. I'm Father John McKenzie, a member of the Chapter of York."

Falcon nodded and closed the study door behind him. He was aware that his father's acquaintances were wide and varied.

He indicated for Father McKenzie to take a seat on one of the small sofas surrounding a coffee table. "Can I get you a drink?"

"No, I'm fine, thank you." The craggy face of the older man creased into a wide smile as he saw the photo of Francis Byrde and his varied group of adopted children which took pride of place on Falcon's sideboard.

"Your father is well?"

"He is." Fal smiled. "He's in Jamaica with my youngest sister Chyna at the moment. They are following up leads on who her birth parents might have been."

Father McKenzie smiled again, then his face became serious as he turned to face Falcon. "What do you know of the Ninth Legion?"

Falcon was surprised by the strange segue. This was why he wanted to talk to him? "Only what everyone knows: they were stationed here in York in the early days of the Roman fortress, then they disappeared from the records and were wiped out." He thought for a moment then added, "I read Rosemary Sutcliffe's *Eagle of the Ninth* when I was young, as many others did."

"Originally, it was assumed that they were defeated in battle in North Britain, or Scotland as we know it, but more recently there have been other theories," said Father McKenzie.

Falcon moved to the front of his seat, intrigued by what the older man was saying. "Why did you come to me?"

"Francis suggested it." he reached into his cassock and withdrew a small coin-like object and passed it to him. It was imprinted with a relief of a peregrine falcon and around the edge were the words *Ordo Avium* – Order of the Birds.

Falcon looked up at the other man. "From Francis?"

Father McKenzie nodded and put the token back in his cassock. "He gave me this years ago when we met up again after school. He moved in some of the more interesting circles that I did."

The younger man nodded. Not too many people outside his family knew about the order. It had been set up by his adopted father when he began his paranormal investigation business. It was a way of guaranteeing the owner a hearing with a member of the team. In this case, that was Falcon.

#

***

Falcon was pulled back to the present when Robin jiggled his shoulder and pointed to a particularly low hanging part of the tunnel. He smiled his thanks at his brother as he lowered his head.

"So," Robin began, "we're on a search for the missing Ninth?"

Chapter Two

Hugh

The café on the corner looked comfortable with both sofas and tables available inside. It was busy, but not too packed that there wasn't anywhere to sit. There were also tables available outside. He approached the counter and almost did a double take. He could swear it was the same girl who had served him in the bookshop.

"Hi," the girl addressed him. "Can I help you?"

"Er, yes. An Americano with milk, please."

She smiled at him as she began making his drink. "I see you've been in the bookshop." She pointed to his book.

"I did. Are you related to Abbie?" It was the only thing he could think of.

"I am, I'm Petronella, but everyone calls me Ella. We're two thirds of triplets, our brother Cory works for Robin in the antiques shop."

"That's handy."

She laughed as she handed him his drink, "Well, our mother Jenny is their sister, they're my uncles."

Having unknowingly dropped that bombshell, she turned to serve the next customer and Hugh made his way outside. There was a sister? He knew they were all adopted children of Francis Byrde, but obviously he didn't know everything.

Picking up his mobile, he pulled up Imogen's contact details:

Did you know there was a sister?

He watched the three little dots for a moment as Imogen wrote her reply.

No. Checking now. I'll get back to you.

Leaving it in Imogen's capable hands, he sipped his drink and looked at the arcade around him. From the information they'd been able to get hold of and local newspaper reports, the whole area had been due for demolition and then rebuilt as flats. Half of it, the part where the arcade had opened onto Blake Street, had already been turned into flats, but the other half, which opened out here onto Stonegate, had been saved from demolition by Francis Byrde.

He'd bought up the remaining shops and had had them updated and owner's flats added onto them. This was where the brothers now lived and traded.

Hugh sat for a while, his book open on the table, half perusing it and half watching the comings and goings of people through the arcade. Ella came out of the café and began clearing tables near him, smiling at him as she passed by.

"Another drink?" she asked. "Thanks. I can order inside?" "It's okay, same again?"

He nodded and she disappeared inside, returning a few moments later with a fresh coffee and a card machine. He tapped his card and thanked her. Just then there was a commotion down the passageway next to him. He could hear swearing and... laughter?

He and Ella both looked up as Falcon Byrde and a younger man came into view. Robin Byrde, Hugh's internal photo album told him. Robin had his older brother's arm slung over his shoulders and was helping to support him, as the older man limped along.

"Uncle Fal!" Ella exclaimed as she went to see if she could help.

"I'm okay, sweetheart," he assured her, grimacing.

Robin was too busy laughing to say anything straightaway, but eventually he got out, "He was too busy making sure I didn't trip that he missed his step and turned his ankle!"

"It's not funny!" Fal grumbled as he allowed his brother to help him towards the bookshop. Ella watched them go until someone call her name, then she went back into the café.

Hugh watched the arcade, but the brothers were in the bookshop now. He would check the camera feed when he got back to his flat later, but for now he could at least listen in on what was being said through the earpiece he was wearing.

"It's not funny!" Hugh recognised Falcon's voice.

"It is a bit funny." Robin's voice replied. "Abbie, be a dear and go get the first aid kit please."

There was silence as Abbie obviously did as she was asked. "What happened?" she asked a few moments later.

"I missed a step," said Falcon.

"He turned round to make sure I was steady on my feet, and twisted his ankle when he turned back," Robin added.

"Really, Uncle Fal!"

"Here," Robin said. "I don't think it's broken."

Hugh pictured him examining Falcon's ankle as it went quiet again. "There. All wrapped up."

"Thanks, Rob."

"Do you need any painkillers?"

"No, I'm okay."

Hugh's phone beeped with an incoming text from Imogen.

Jenny Byrde married Foster Green 20 years ago and they have triplets Abbie, Petronella and Cory who all work in the shops in the Arcade. They're 18. Not much is known about her. I'll keep looking.

I've met the girls. Abbie works in the bookshop and Petronella (Ella) in the café. I believe the boy Cory works in the antique shop.

He waited a moment, but nothing else came through from Imogen. Putting his phone away, he listened in on the earpiece, but all he could hear was Abbie talking to customers. The brothers must have moved into the back where Falcon's office was.

Draining his drink, Hugh stood up, waved goodbye to Ella then left the arcade. He headed down Stonegate, walking past several shops including the York Roast shop. He sniffed appreciatively when he passed, promising himself he'd get lunch from there one day. Other shops included clothes shops, souvenir shops and more eateries. A street of one kind or another had been on the same spot since Roman times. He turned right onto Blake Street, with its more modern shop fronts, then a few moments later, he entered the front room of his rented maisonette and threw the keys into a bowl on the sideboard.

The first thing he did was switch on his laptop and bring up the camera feed from the bookshop. Apart from being able to see what had been happening, there was nothing different to what he'd heard. After Robin had strapped his brother's ankle up, he and Fal had moved to the back of the shop, leaving Abbie in charge once more.

Hugh's phone rang. He recognised the ring tone as Imogen's. "What have you got for me?" he asked without preamble.

"And hello to you too!"

"Imogen!"

There was a huff from the other end of the phone. "I checked up on the family. Apart from the boys we already knew about, there are two sisters, Jenny and Chyna."

"Chyna?"

"Yes, she's in Jamaica at the moment with Francis Byrde. From what I was able to find out, they're there to try and track down some of Chyna's biological family."

"Interesting," he mused. "That's why he's not around at the moment. Anyone else we've missed?"

"Not that I know of," replied Imogen.

"Make sure," he instructed.

Imogen huffed again and put the phone down.

Hugh stretched and wandered over to the window that looked down on the arcade, where he could keep an eye on the bookshop. He watched as Abbie locked up the shop and joined a young boy who was just coming out of the antiques shop. That should in theory be her brother. When they were joined by Ella, he knew he was right.

He mooched around the maisonette's kitchen, making himself some steamed salmon and green beans for dinner. He could have gone out – there were several excellent restaurants around where he was – but he fancied a home cooked meal.

#

The next few days passed in a pattern. Hugh spent the mornings catching up on videos from the bookshop from the previous day. With only the one camera, he wasn't catching too much. He spent the rest of the time trying to work out what Falcon Byrde was up to and investigating the rest of the brothers.

He was looking through the scope at the shop when Falcon left, on his own and heading for Stonegate. Making a quick decision, Hugh threw on a canvas jacket as it had been raining earlier, and ran down the stairs and out the door. Rounding the corner to Stonegate, he caught a sight of his quarry as he stopped to chat with someone outside Ye Olde Starre Inn, the oldest pub in the area.

Hugh stopped a few shops up and waited. Falcon slapped the other man on the shoulder, giving a great guffaw of laughter, and then moved on at a good clip down Stonegate and into Minster Gate. Falcon then joined an older man dressed in a black cassock who was waiting for him on the steps of the Minster leading to the side door. Hugh managed to get a photograph of them and sent it to Imogen to see if she could find out who he was.

There were benches in Dean's Park and it was a warmish May day, so he settled down on one, bringing out the book he'd been reading as a cover in case he needed it.

His phone buzzed with a text. It was Imogen.

* * *

That's Father McKenzie. He's attached to the Charter House at the Minster.

Why would he be meeting Falcon Byrde?

No information on that. McKenzie's as clean as a whistle. Nothing on him, not even a speeding ticket.

Okay, thanks. I'll stick around a bit longer and let you know if anything happens.

He put his phone away and contemplated what he knew already about Falcon Byrde. Nothing made any kind of sense, yet his boss was convinced he was negatively involved in the Goodkind killings.

There was no denying Falcon had been there when the Goodkind family had been killed. Their business premises had been blown up and Falcon had been one of the people to call 999 and had tried to give first aid to some of the passersby. It would all seem coincidental – being in the wrong place at the wrong time – if it weren't for the fact that was the fourth time he'd been in the wrong place at the wrong time in the last couple of years.

It had been enough to persuade Robert Swales that he was involved in some nefarious way. Hugh had to admit he had his doubts. There was nothing he'd come across so far that gave any credence to Swales's suspicions. That alone was beginning to trigger Hugh's alarms.

Falcon

* * *

Falcon was pleased that his ankle was no longer bothering him. It had been inconvenient when it happened, and he had been embarrassed. More so that it had happened when Robin had been with him. He was always more aware of where they were putting their feet when his little brother was with him. Though Falcon knew that the younger man didn't have any problems with walking, he still wanted to make sure he was able to get around okay.

It was a sunny Wednesday morning, and he had an appointment to meet with Father McKenzie at the Charterhouse at the Minster. It was nearing 11am when he said goodbye to Abbie and headed off down Stonegate. He was pleased to see Arne who was the publican at Ye Olde Starre Inn. They'd been friends for years, and it was nice to catch up.

Laughing as he left his old friend, he quickly made his way to the Minster, happy to see that Father McKenzie was waiting for him.

"Come in, come in!" McKenzie welcomed him with a smile.

The soaring ceiling and architecture was amazing and Falcon was caught up, as always, in the majesty of the building. He followed McKenzie through to a small side room, which appeared to be a kind of robing room. Through another door was a small area with a kitchen and McKenzie asked if he wanted a drink.

"Coffee please." He made small talk whilst McKenzie made the coffee, then they settled in the larger room where many cassocks, surplices and vestments were stored.

"Take a seat."

Falcon sat down on a ratty sofa, which turned out to be very comfy. He put his mug down on the coffee table in front of him.

"How's the ankle?" Father McKenzie asked as they settled in.

"A lot better, thanks. Such a stupid thing to do."

The other man laughed and nodded. "Remind me to tell you about the time I broke my leg stepping off a train."

"Really, just from stepping off a train?"

"Turns out I have brittle bones."

Falcon just shook his head and slowly sipped his coffee as he contemplated what to tell the older man. They hadn't exactly found a great deal before he'd twisted his ankle.

"I've had a word with the manager at the Treasurer's House and she's agreed to let you into the cellar that Harry Martindale saw the ghost Roman soldiers marching through in 1953. There has always been speculation that they were some of the remnants of the Ninth Legion returning to York in defeat," said McKenzie.

"I've read that story. There was an article on Martindale in the York Press in 2014 when he died. I've also done some reading around it." Falcon grinned. "One of the perks of owning a bookshop."

"Myrna, the National Trust manager in charge of the Treasurer's House will let you in after the last tour has gone through about 4.30 pm. You'll need to contact her to arrange a date."

Falcon nodded and finished his coffee. "You know I'm not convinced we're actually talking about *the* Ninth Legion, don't you?"

"I'm not either. But I know what I saw in that room."

Falcon nodded again. He'd have to go back and have another look himself. He'd find a different way into the old hewn out room with round Roman shields and weapons hanging on its bare walls that Father McKenzie claimed to have found. Apparently, other memorabilia hung around the room, some of it with the distinctive IX Legio Hisp mark on them. The question they were trying to answer was were they from the real legion – although surely the wooden shields would have deteriorated by now – or were they false? Father McKenzie had been a young man when he saw them and had not been allowed to follow up then. His higher ups had forbidden it. Now they were long gone, and he had the authority to institute the investigation.

"Who else here knows about the tunnels?" Falcon asked.

McKenzie went quiet. "I've kept it fairly close. Only a couple of other people in my office know about it, even then, they don't know where the entrances I found are."

"I'll be returning to the tunnels later this week," Falcon informed Father McKenzie. "I'll make sure I'm better prepared this time."

The older man nodded and they finished their meeting.

Falcon followed Father McKenzie outside and waved to him as he walked back down Minster Yard. As he did so, he noticed a man sitting on a bench with a book beside him. He recognised the book; he had a couple of copies in his shop. It was a local history of York looking at the many, many ghost stories that were prevalent in the area. He smiled, sure this was the man both Ella and Abbie had described to him. They'd been giggling at the time and he hadn't taken their matchmaking seriously.

Now though, looking at the man, he could see why they'd mentioned him. He was definitely his type. He hoped he'd come into the bookshop again whilst he was there.

With nothing more serious on his mind, Falcon made his way back to the shop. He let himself into his study and began catching up on emails and messages. He grinned when he noticed one from his adopted father, Francis.

Hi Fal. You'll be pleased to hear that Chyna is settled at university and already making friends. We didn't find any relatives, but we went into this knowing we probably wouldn't. I'll be on my way back in the next couple of days and can't wait to hear what you've been up to! A little bird (Robin) told me about your latest venture and the ankle. Hope it's all cleared up now. You can update me on John's request when I'm back in York.

I'll make sure to invite you all for dinner. Love always

Dad

Falcon rolled his eyes at the message. Of course Robin had been sneaky and told their father what was happening. Still, Francis had many years of experience to bring to the mystery.

There was also a quick message from Father McKenzie giving him contact details for Myrna Hopkins so he could arrange a date to visit the Treasurer's House cellar. He decided he'd wait to revisit the tunnels until after that. Francis might be home by then and he could come with him.

Chapter Three

Hugh

Hugh watched Falcon as he came out of the Minster and waved goodbye to the man in the cassock. Leaving it a few moments, he followed after Falcon as he made his way back to his bookshop.

Letting himself into the maisonette half an hour later, he put his bag of groceries down on the kitchen table after stocking up at Tesco. He was in the process of putting everything away when his phone rang.

It was Swales. Hugh squinted at the phone; it wasn't often he spoke to the big man himself.

"This is McHughes," he answered.

"McHughes, Swales here." Hugh squinted, as if he couldn't see it was him. "Yes, sir?" he answered.

"How are you proceeding?"

"I've been following Falcon Byrde and his brothers for a couple of weeks now, and honestly, I haven't come across anything that connects them to the attack on the Goodkind family."

Swales harrumphed and Hugh held the phone away from his ear. He wasn't impressed.

"Sir?"

"What about this religious man he's cosying up with?"

"Father McKenzie. From what I can find out he's attached to the Chapter House at York Minster, though I don't yet know why he's meeting with Byrde."

"Then find out!" The other man growled at him. "I want that man eliminated! Really, McHughes, do I need to do your job for you?"

Hugh realised Swales had put the phone down on him and he frowned.

Eliminated? That was never his job. What did he really know about the man he called Boss?

He texted Imogen.

Just had the pleasure of a call from Swales.

Her reply was almost immediate.

Lucky for you.

Yeah, wouldn't exactly call it lucky. What's his beef?

Meet me from the 5.50pm train and we'll have dinner.

Imogen?

Just meet me, Hugh.

Okay, I'll be there.

* * *

More confused, Hugh finished putting his groceries away, then returned to the scope he'd set up in the front room. Something strange was definitely going on. He'd seen Falcon go into the shop and through to the back area through his camera. He weighed up the possibility of getting in there to plant more cameras and bugs, but he couldn't see a way to do it covertly.

He had just over a couple of hours before Imogen arrived. He had time to go for another mooch around the bookshop anyway. He'd practically finished reading the book he'd bought, and wondered if they had anything on the Ninth Legion or the Romans in York. He'd been fascinated by them since he was a child and had read Rosemary Sutcliffe's *Eagle of the Ninth*. Maybe they'd have a copy of that?

Making a decision, he grabbed his jacket again and headed out.

#

Abbie was behind the counter in the bookshop again and she beamed at him. "Hello, you came back!"

"I did!"

She just laughed at him.

"I'm off to look around the history section." He began moving off, then stopped. "Hey, Abbie?"

"Yeah?"

"Do you know if you've got a copy of Rosemary Sutcliffe's *Eagle of the Ninth*?" She scrunched up her face as she thought. "Let me just check the inventory."

"It's okay, Abbie. I can help." A masculine voice sounded from behind him. Hugh turned around to see Falcon Byrde eyeing him quizzically. He was entering the shop from the back rooms and looked delicious to Hugh's eyes. Wearing indigo jeans and a dark blue t-shirt with the shop logo on, he was beautiful. Realising he'd missed what Falcon had asked him, Hugh asked him to repeat it.

"I asked if you'd asked after *The Eagle of the Ninth*?"

"Yeah, I remember reading it as a child and thought whilst I was in York for a couple of months, I'd revisit it. Seeing as this is supposed to be the last place they were seen."

"We don't have it." Abbie looked up from her computer. "But we can order it in for you."

"No, it's okay, Abbie," he replied. "It was just a thought." Hugh was surprised when Falcon next spoke.

"I have a copy you could borrow." "No, really, it's okay."

Falcon grinned and held his hand out. "I've not introduced myself properly yet.

I'm Falcon Byrde, I own the shop."

"Hugh McHughes," he replied, holding his own hand out. He jumped as he got a slight static shock from the other man.

He looked at Falcon, noticing how his eyes were a warm brown colour and that his whole face lit up when he smiled.

"Well, if you're sure you don't mind, I could borrow your copy."

"Sure, no problem. It might take me awhile to dig it out though. Why don't I bring it to you over dinner tonight?"

Hot damn! Hugh thought. *Trust Imogen to get in my way.*

"I'd love that, but my friend will be arriving soon and I have to go meet her from the train."

Falcon looked disappointed and took a slight step back.

"No, really. If Imogen wasn't coming through especially to meet me, I'd definitely take you up on your offer."

Falcon gave him that blinding smile again. "Why don't

you give me your email and phone number, then I can let you know when I've found it? We can make dinner plans at the same time."

Hugh agreed. Taking his phone from his pocket, he added Falcon's details to his contacts. He buzzed a message off to the Falcon's phone.

"Now you have mine as well."

They stood there smiling at each other with Abbie giggling near the till. Hugh jumped and looked at the time on his phone: 5.40 pm. Imogen's train would be in soon. He'd best get a move on.

"I…" he began, reddening slightly at his attraction to the other man. "I really have to be going. She'll kick me if I'm late."

Falcon and Abbie laughed.

"We can't have that. I'll phone you when I find the book," said Falcon.

"Book?" Hugh asked. Then groaned. "Yes, of course. See you."

Quickly making his way out of the bookshop, Hugh groaned again. He couldn't believe what an ass he'd made of himself. Not that he should be getting involved anyway – he was there to do a job, not make friends.

#

He arrived at the railway station with a small amount of time to spare. Checking which platform Imogen's train would be coming in on, he saw it had already arrived. No point in going any further. He scoured the crowds for her, then noticed her approaching him. She was dressed in a rich red trouser suit, with the jacket open to show the cream camisole she wore underneath it. The colour really suited her. He reached her and leaned down to kiss her cheek. He'd known Imogen ever since he'd started working for the agency, and they'd become fast friends.

"I've not seen this before," he said, gesturing to her suit. "The colour really suits

you."

She returned his kiss, then took hold of his hand and began walking out of the

station.

"Bit of retail therapy. You'll understand when I explain over dinner. Where are we going?" she asked as they negotiated their way past the evening commuters.

"I thought we'd try *The Judge's Lodging*. It's supposed to have excellent food."

"And excellent cocktails?" she asked.

"I don't know."

"God, I hope so, I could do with a good cocktail!"

"Going to tell me what's going on, Imogen?"

"Not yet, let's have dinner first."

He sighed but turned them down Lendal after they crossed the river. The building was on their left and Hugh knew it had once been used as accommodation for the judges at the Assizes in York and still had many of its original features.

There were plenty of tables available in the courtyard as it was still early. They settled at one and picked up the menus in front of them.

"May I take your drink order?" A young man stood by the side of the table, tablet in hand.

"I'll have a Cosmopolitan and a glass of water," Imogen ordered.

"And you, sir?"

"Just water for me, please."

The waiter nodded. He told them he'd be back to take their food orders shortly, then left them to their menus.

"Have you decided?" Imogen asked him, looking up from her menu.

"I have, you?"

She nodded and when the waiter returned with their drinks, they put their food order in. Imogen took a grateful sip of her Cosmopolitan and closed her eyes, savouring it.

"That bad?" Hugh asked, only then taking in the dark shadows under her eyes, which hadn't been there the other day. "What gives, Imogen?"

She sighed, playing with her glass for a time. "Things at the office are spiraling out of control."

He leaned towards her. "In what way?"

"Swales has not been seen for several days now. Neither in the office nor at his home. His wife said he was in Berlin on business, but there's no record of him leaving the country. So when you messaged and said he'd spoken directly to you, I knew there was something more to it."

Hugh frowned. He was a field agent and rarely in the office, so didn't interact with Swales as much as the office staff did. Imogen was his go between, his research agent and backup.

Imogen drew breath as though she were going to ask him a question. Before she could, the fire alarm began going off. Even though they were sitting outside, the staff told them to evacuate the area. Hugh could barely hear himself think and looked around him as people began muttering and moving away, though they only went as far as the street.

Hugh noticed that there was a plume of smoke emerging

from the kitchen to the right of the building and wasn't surprised when the door opened and several members of staff began spilling out, several of them coughing because of the smoke.

"Please, everyone!" shouted the waiter who had served them. Some of the other staff were asking the small crowd of onlookers to move further away so the fire engines could get in when they arrived. Hugh could already hear their distinctive wail getting closer.

Hugh grabbed Imogen's hand and began moving with her further away from the hotel. There were more people out in the street now, as residents began swelling the ranks of the patrons from the courtyard. He found himself being pushed and shoved and he lost his hold on Imogen's hand.

"Not you, Mr McHughes." The voice was barely recognisable, but Hugh swore it belonged to Swales. "You're coming with me."

Hugh went to turn around, then he felt something press into his back. The man behind him was holding a gun. He went very still and allowed himself to be manoeuvered away from the crowd and towards the main road.

"Don't struggle. I'd hate to have to use a weapon in this crowd."

Hugh remained silent, cursing all the way as he was thrust in front of the other man. He followed the direction and found himself out on Museum Street. He was pushed towards a Land Rover parked across the entrance to the Museum Gardens. No-one was paying them any attention; they were too busy gawking at the fire engines as they pulled onto Lendal to *The Judge's Lodging*. Feeling more hands on him, he realised the man with the gun was not on his own.

"Give us your phone," a gruff voice insisted.

Hugh tried to resist as one of them reached into his pocket and drew out his phone, throwing it as far as he could into the gardens. Thankfully, he missed hitting any pedestrian.

"Get in the car."

He again tried to fight against the other men, but he was outnumbered. Suddenly, he felt a blow to his temple, and he pulled back from the pain. Stumbling from the dizziness, he was shoved into the back of the Land Rover. Collapsing on the back seat, he tried to stay awake, but his last thought as he slipped into unconsciousness was that he must have been hit harder than he realised.

#

Hugh came back to consciousness slowly. His head ached and he could feel blood trickling down his cheek. He knew he was still in the back of the Land Rover, though he couldn't see out of the windows as he had been shoved unceremoniously onto the floor and a jacket or something thrown over him. He tried not to stir, not wanting to let his captors know he was awake. He had no idea how long he'd been out.

The vehicle slowed and the front driver's window was lowered. There was a quiet conversation and then they were moving again.

The back door opened, and he was roughly grabbed by one of the goons.

"Get out," he growled at him.

Hugh slowly backed out of the Land Rover, his head throbbing. He felt nauseous and without warning, he turned round and was sick at the man's feet. The heavyset man wearing a red parka grumbled as he jumped back.

"Bring him," the other goon, who had a nasty looking scar across his face, commanded. The third man, who he thought was Swales, had already disappeared.

Red parka and Scarface pulled Hugh along between them. Hugh dragged his feet as much as he could, but he couldn't stop them pulling him into the house they'd stopped at.

The third man, definitely Swales, Hugh recognised him, was waiting for them in the hallway. "Parkin," he addressed Scarface, "put him in the attic room."

Parkin nodded and dragged Hugh off. He tried to protest, but his head was still

groggy from having been knocked out and he didn't have his full strength.

At the top of a narrow flight of stairs, Hugh was roughly shoved into a room, which had a bed, a dressing table and a couple of doors off. He turned round to hear Parkin locking the door behind him. He collapsed onto the bed, groaning. His head was aching, but he still felt a little nauseous. He got off the bed and opened one of the doors, which was just a cupboard. The other door led to a small bathroom.

After being sick in the toilet, he flushed and looked around. There was a small glass standing by the sink. He filled it with water and rinsed his mouth out. Refilling the glass, he returned to the main room to have a look around. He looked out the window, but it didn't give him any real clues as to where he was. With nothing else going on he laid back on the bed. Wishing he had some pain killers for his head, he closed his eyes and rested. There was nothing he could do until someone came to his room.

#

* * *

Falcon

Falcon felt as though he was floating. He was being carried down a white corridor, his mind roaming free. He watched as the fluorescent lights went by one-by-one overhead. Falcon tried to count them but kept losing where he was up to.

He was dressed in his pyjamas, and the orderly carrying him was being as gentle as he could, but he was still working for the facility. Falcon's mind felt as though it was detached from the rest of him.

Minutes later, he was deposited fairly tenderly on his bed in the dorm room. His head was still spinning, and it took a few moments before he felt the room stop whirling around him.

He knew it was the drugs, and he hated it. Hated every time they gave him a new experimental drug and put him through the tests. His body felt as though he was being pummeled through the mattress and he slowly tried to sit up.

He felt the bed give and looked over at his little brother Robin. The little boy was missing his legs below his knees. He'd been like that for a few years now. Ever since he'd gotten sepsis in his lower legs after a procedure gone wrong in another experiment.

Robin bounced on his knees on the bed. He was mostly confined to his wheelchair but had learned to use his knees to move around independently. He felt Falcon's forehead with his little hand and stroked through his hair. Falcon knew he was copying what he himself did when any of them were ill.

Pip sat on the bed next to him. He was next in age to Falcon and helped him look out for the others. He considered them all his brothers and sisters, but none of them were actually related.

#

Falcon drew in a deep breath and sat up suddenly. He

couldn't remember much of the dream, only that it had been about their time in the facility. He tried not to let the memories and nightmares get to him as much now that he was older. He was just forever glad that they'd escaped from that. All with the help of Francis Byrde. Their saviour had come in and adopted all eight children at the facility, from Falcon who'd been 17 at the time, down to Robin who was only 8 years old.

He felt his heart beating quickly and he gulped in a few more deep breaths. To try and divert his thoughts, he brought up the memory of Hugh McHughes. The man fascinated him. He hadn't met a man before who attracted him as much as Hugh did.

After getting up and getting himself a drink of water, he settled back in bed and was finally able to fall back to sleep without any more dreams.

The early morning found him in that in-between place, not awake and not asleep.

He sent his mind and senses out until he felt a connection.

#

He soared high over the city. The whole of York was laid out below him and he followed the winding River Ouse as it ran through the city. His eyes were now a lot sharper than his human ones, as he watched the world below as a lark.

He loved having the freedom to connect with the birds. To follow where they flew and see out of their eyes. He was able to exert a little control over where the bird went, and he directed the lark to swoop down towards the courtyard where he now lived. It was early, but already people were up and out, going about their morning activities. Some going to jobs, others to school. The less fortunate were rolling up the sleeping bags they'd spent the night in – if they were lucky enough to have one – and putting them away ready for another day on the streets of the tourist city.

He directed the lark to dip and dive around the cathedral, enjoying the feeling it transported to him as he lay in his bed. Deans Park and the roads around it were his playground and he spend the next half hour or so just enjoying his connection to the wild bird flying free.

#

Falcon awoke properly when his mobile phone began ringing. He grinned; it was Francis's ring tone. Reaching over to his bedside table, he picked it up.

"Hey, Dad. You home?"

"Got in late last night," Francis Byrde replied. "Wondered if you wanted to get coffee later today?"

"Sounds great. Meet you at the café about 11 am?"

After a few more pleasantries, Falcon ended the call and got out of bed. He wanted to see if he could find his copy of *The Eagle of the Ninth* today; he'd promised Hugh he'd look it out. It would also give him an excuse to see him again. Maybe even invite him out for dinner?

A couple of hours later, he walked through the bookshop on his way out to the café.

"How's it going, Abbie?" he asked his niece who was sitting at the computer and sending out invoices.

"Great, Uncle Fal. Been a bit quiet today, so I'm catching up on some admin." "Good girl. I'm off to meet your granddad."

Abbie whooped. "He's back?"

"Got in last night. I'll make sure he comes to visit you before he leaves."

Abbie grinned. Falcon knew that Francis made a great grandfather and the triplets loved him. He said his goodbyes and headed over to the café.

As he walked in, Francis was being crushed in hug by Ella. She was grinning from ear to ear and only broke off when she spotted Falcon.

"Hey there, Uncle Fal. Usual?"

He nodded and she went off to make their drinks. He greeted his father with a hearty hug. He'd missed him more than he thought he would. Francis returned the hug, then turned and led the way to one of the comfy sofas in the coffee shop.

When their drinks came, they spent a little time chatting about Chyna and how she was settling in at university in Jamaica. Francis thought she'd be very happy there and Fal hoped so as his youngest sister had always wanted to live in and go to university in the Caribbean.

"So..." Francis paused to sip his drink. "How are things going with Father John McKenzie?"

"Hmm," Fal murmured. "I told you about the research I've been doing? I'm not convinced it's the actual Ninth Legion we're talking about, and nor is McKenzie. But there is something going on, that's for sure. Some of those tunnels, including the one we entered, are lethal." He grimaced, remembering his injured ankle.

"They're strange. They're definitely old, though I'm not sure just how old. Some parts of them were really rough and others reminded me more of Flemish brick work. As though they'd been updated at some time."

"A conundrum," Francis said. "When do you intend to go again?"

Before he had a chance to answer, there was a commotion

at the door. A young blonde-haired woman dressed in a red crumpled trouser suit was trying to get to the front of the queue.

"Excuse me, sorry," she said as she made her way to where Ella was serving.

"I'm so sorry," she repeated. "But have you seen Hugh today?"

Ella frowned as she shook her head.

Falcon stood up and walked up to the young woman. "Hugh McHughes?" he asked.

She turned around towards him. He took in her dishevelled stated and wondered what had happened. He ordered her a chamomile tea and took her over to where Francis was sitting.

"Here," he helped her sit down. "I haven't seen him since yesterday. Are you the friend he was meeting for dinner?"

She nodded and held out her hand. "Imogen Lovell."

Falcon introduced himself and Francis then sat down. "Can you tell us what happened?

"We went for a drink and dinner at *The Judge's Lodging,* after he met me from my train."

Falcon nodded at her to continue. Slowly, Imogen told them about the fire alarm and about losing track of Hugh in the melee. Then she told them how she'd not been able to find him afterwards. He wasn't at the maisonette he was staying in and there had been no sign of him since then.

"I spent the night there, but didn't get much sleep. I was hoping he'd turn up there. I've no idea what to do now. I went back to the restaurant this morning and no- one even remembered us being there. It was chaos after the fire alarm went off, but no- one recognised my description of the waiter who served us." She twisted her hands in her lap and shook her head in frustration.

"Hey, hey, it'll be okay," Falcon said, attempting to comfort her.

"Something is obviously happening," Francis mused. "What can you tell us about him?"

Imogen took in a deep breath and looked at the person they'd been sent to spy on. Then, taking a chance, she told them everything she knew about what Hugh was doing in York.

Chapter Four

Hugh

Hugh was pacing. Six steps to the door, turn, six steps to the window, then six more steps back to the wall where the bed was. On repeat. He'd lost count of the number of times he'd repeated his route after he became aware that he was being watched through the window.

On the ledge, on the other side of the barred window, sat three birds: a robin, a blackbird and a crow. They all watched him, their heads cocked to one side. Hugh was freaked out. When did birds act like that in synchronisation? He shook his head, convinced he was still affected by the blow he'd taken. He closed his eyes and then opened them again. The three birds were still there.

He moved closer to the window. He'd looked at it when he'd been first shoved into the attic, looking for a way out. Beyond the window were overgrown gardens and a boundary wall, upon which sat about twenty more birds, all different sizes and species. Weird.

Looking further he could see they were on the top of a rise, and he could just make out the woods around the property. They were in the countryside somewhere, but he didn't think it was too far from York, as they hadn't been in the Land Rover that long.

Some of the birds took off from the boundary wall and others appeared to take their place. The three on the window ledge continued to watch him, heads cocked.

There was a noise at the door and Hugh turned towards it. One of Swales's goons entered and smirked at Hugh. In his hand he held a taser. Hugh swallowed. He'd been tased before and it hadn't been a pleasant experience.

"Mr. Swales wants to see you." The goon gestured with the taser for Hugh to go in front of him before shoving him roughly down two flights of stairs. Hugh barely managed to keep his feet under him. Then he was propelled into a side room, where Swales was sitting drinking tea at the table.

"Ah, Hugh. So glad you could join us."

Swales gestured to the other side of the table, but Hugh shook his head. The goon shoved him in the back, so Hugh moved over and reluctantly sat down.

"Thank you, Bentley." Swales motioned for the other man to go stand by the door. Hugh knew the taser could reach him from there, so he kept a wary eye on him.

"What's going on, Swales? Why the kidnapping?" he asked.

"You weren't doing your job. Falcon Byrde should have been dead by now."

Hugh looked at him in confusion. The job had been to keep an eye on Falcon and find out if he was involved in what had happened to the Goodkind family, not to take him out without prejudice.

"That was never in my instructions!" he protested. "No? I

seem to recall telling you to take the initiative."

"That doesn't mean to kill someone willy nilly!" he roared, half getting out of his seat. Bentley moved forward menacingly, and Hugh sat back down.

"You're mad!"

Swales just sipped his tea, buttered a crumpet and took a big bite out of it. After swallowing, he gave his attention to Hugh once more.

"No. I think the word you're looking for is psychopath," he said calmly.

Hugh blinked and looked at his boss. This was so weird. Though he didn't know Swales that well, he could swear that he was dealing with a completely different person. His eyes narrowed as he really looked at the man sitting across from him.

"You're not Robert Swales," he declared finally.

"Give the man a prize." Not-Swales gave him a slow clap. "Took you long enough. I thought you were the best?"

Hugh shook his head in disbelief. What was going on here?

"Who are you then?" he asked.

"Ian Swales at your service. Well, not really." He giggled. Giggled! Hugh was beginning to think the man was deranged.

"You're Robert's brother?"

"Twin actually," the other man answered. "Don't worry, Robert is perfectly well. He's having a well-deserved rest at a secure and restful sanatorium. The staff have been told he's under the impression he's Robert when he's actually Ian."

"That's..." Hugh had no words. The man was certifiably mad.

"What do you want?" he decided to try and get to the bottom of what was happening.

"I want you to kill Falcon Byrde."

"Why?"

"He's in my way."

"That's not a good enough reason to kill him. I'm not doing your dirty work for you!"

"You will kill him!" Ian roared, launching himself out of his seat and clearing the table with a sweep of his arm. "No! You can't make me."

Ian grinned. He gestured to Bentley who, without warning, shot Hugh with the taser. Hugh gasped and arched his body as he felt the electricity shoot through him. He slipped off the chair until he was lying beside it in a sprawl.

"Put him back in the attic," Ian said, back to acting like the suave man he'd appeared to be at first. "I need to get back to the office and catch up with little Imogen."

Hugh felt blackness surround him. "No..." he whispered, trying to speak. "Leave..."

"What was that?" Ian smiled at him as he stepped over Hugh and headed for the door.

A couple of moments later, Bentley picked him up and slung him over his shoulder. Hugh hung there, swearing inside. He'd not recovered enough from being tasered yet to take Bentley down. All he could do was hang there and moan.

Bentley unceremoniously dumped him on the bed in the attic room, and Hugh sprawled there. He tried to turn over and groaned as his limbs began to come back online. Pins and needles made their way down his arms and legs, and he shuddered. He hated being helpless like this. His mind was churning. He'd not known that Robert Swales had a twin brother. He'd never heard of Ian before. Robert had obviously kept that close to his chest.

He groaned again as he turned over, pulling himself up to sit against the headboard. He managed to grab the glass of water that he'd left on the bedside cabinet.

He took a grateful sip of water, before putting it back down again.

As he turned his head, he noticed that there were still three birds lined up on his windowsill, though they were different from earlier. This time there was a pigeon, a swallow and a blackbird. All watching him with their heads cocked to one side. What the hell was going on?

Feeling the effects of the taser still running through his system, Hugh gave into exhaustion and fell asleep on the bed.

#

A couple of hours later, Hugh awoke to a hear loud noise that sounded like things crashing together. He shot off the bed, grateful his body felt okay again.

He could hear shouting and more noises, but then it all went quiet. Quickly, he looked around the room for anything he could use as a weapon. He wasn't sure what was going on, but he would rather be prepared than not. There was nothing that he could use though. He quickly moved behind the door; maybe he could take whoever it was by surprise when they entered the room.

There were sounds on the stairs and then the door was thrust open. Hugh tensed, ready to attack Bentley or another of Swales's goons when to his surprise, Falcon Byrde came through the door. He drew back his fist just in time to avoid hitting the other man in the face.

"What the hell?" he asked.

Falcon looked at him and smiled. "Good to see you're in

one piece."

Hugh shook his head. What? How?

"Hugh!" That was Imogen's voice. How was she here?

"Oh, thank god you're okay," she said as she entered the room, flinging herself into his arms. He held her close, feeling her trembling as they hugged tightly.

"Sorry," she mumbled into his chest. "It's been a hard couple of days."

Hugh could only nod and take in the sight of Falcon Byrde, and another man he'd not seen before who was standing in the corridor.

"Francis Byrde." The tall, red-haired man held his hand out for Hugh to shake. "How did you find me?" he asked as they made their way downstairs.

"Let's just say a little bird told us where you were." Falcon grinned at him as they entered the lobby.

Hugh turned to look at him, but at that moment, another of the brothers – Ollie, Hugh thought – approached them.

"All clear," he said.

"No sign of Swales?" Francis asked. Ollie shook his head.

"I've no idea what he's playing at." Imogen twined her arm with one of Hugh's. "Did he say anything to you, Hugh?"

He turned to face them all and grimaced. "That was not Robert Swales."

"What?" Imogen stared at him. "What do you mean?"

"That was his psychopathic twin, Ian Swales."

Imogen gaped at him. "But… but…"

"Yeah, I know. Took me by surprise as well."

"Then where's our boss?"

"In some sanatorium somewhere under Ian's name."

"Shit." Francis Byrde came to stand near them. "Ian's on the loose again?"

"You know him?" Hugh asked stunned.

"Knew him." Francis replied. "I was at school with both Robert and Ian. Let's just say Ian and I never got along. He was always a bit off. It wasn't until later when he killed a man and was sent to a secure psychiatric hospital that we all realised just how ill he was."

Hugh shook his head. "Why target Falcon then? Why not you?"

"How do you mean, target me?" Falcon asked.

"He was most insistent that you were in his way. He was practically foaming at the mouth and shouting at me to kill you."

Falcon turned white and Hugh ached to reach out to comfort him. Francis drew in a breath. "I can't think of any reason why he'd want my son dead."

Hugh shook his head. What a mess.

"Okay," Ollie said, "the police are on their way to take the 'help' into custody. Let's get out of here, while we still can."

Hugh followed them out into a large courtyard, where two black SUVs were parked. He and Imogen got into the one driven by Falcon and as Hugh slid into his seat, he could see dozens of birds take off into the sky and disappear.

Something strange was going on with that. He shook his head, too tired to think about it now. He'd think about it when they got back to York.

#

Falcon

They were sitting at one of the tables in the courtyard of *The Judge's Lodging*. Francis joined them with an older woman in tow. She was wearing the uniform of the hotel reception staff and looked concerned.

"This is Paula, she's the day manager on duty. I've given her the description of the waiter you gave me, Imogen."

The woman turned to them and shook her head. "It doesn't match the description of any of the waiters or bar staff we employ. We've found out this morning that the fire in the kitchen yesterday was set deliberately."

After a couple more minutes of her apologising to them for the disruption the previous evening and giving them some money off vouchers for future use, she went back up the outside stairs to reception.

"I don't understand," Hugh said to Francis.

"Swales must have been following you. He probably acted on the spur of the moment and inserted the young man as a waiter. How many other people were around? Were there many staff?"

"Only about half a dozen tables were taken," Imogen replied. "I don't remember seeing any other staff outside."

Falcon looked to the large building that housed *The Judge's Lodging and Cellar Bar.* There was still soot around one of the windows in the kitchen. They'd been told they were only serving drinks until the kitchen was cleared. It made sense; smoke from fires could cause a lot of damage and take some time to be cleared up.

"Is there anyone in your agency you can trust with investigating this?" Francis asked her.

Imogen shook her head. "There aren't many of us to begin with, and most are out on assignment. There's usually only myself and Peter in the office, along with Swales, though he's been absent more than usual recently."

"You could ask Gil," Hugh said. "I think he's finished his last assignment."

Imogen slowly nodded. "It's a possibility. I'll phone him later."

"Can you go back to the office and try and access any relevant records?" Falcon asked her.

Imogen sighed. Reaching into her bag, she pulled out her smart phone and opened it for Francis and Falcon to see. She showed them the email she'd received from Swales that morning telling her she was fired and not to go near the office if she wanted to avoid legal action being taken against her.

"So that's it," she said when they gave her the phone back. "I'm shut out, I can't even access the computers remotely as I usually do."

Francis shook his head. "You're forgetting that wasn't your boss who sent that. That was Ian."

Imogen looked at Francis, her eyes big, then she grinned. "Good point. I thought there was something odd going on with Swales. He's being acting strangely for the last couple of months. Sending people on jobs we wouldn't normally take. Gil, the agent Hugh just mentioned, refused a job recently, stating it wasn't within the agency's parameters."

Hugh interjected a comment here and there but admitted that he hardly knew Swales and that Imogen saw the most of him. Falcon watched Hugh as he sat nursing a mineral water. He was fascinated by the other man, even knowing he'd been sent there to spy on him. He thought back to his search for Hugh earlier that day.

#

He was soaring high above York again. This time he was looking out through the eyes of a swallow who was dipping and diving, searching for its dinner. From there he moved further out, spreading his senses as far as he could, connecting with several birds at once. He asked for them to look for the man whose picture he thrust into their minds. He flew with many around the York area, moving east, west, south and north. He really hoped that Hugh was nearby, that he had not been moved far. Reports from his contacts started to come back to him. They weren't in words as such, mostly pictures, but he understood what they were telling him.

Nothing. Nothing. Nothing. Nothing. Something?

That report was from three birds: a robin, a blackbird and a crow. He concentrated on them and followed them to an old house to the north of York. Near Earswick. No, further north than that. Haxby?

It was hard to get exact destinations from the birds as they didn't use road maps as humans did and didn't know nor care about the names of places. It was landmarks which Falcon recognised that led him to the areas where these three birds were.

He found himself looking in through three different pairs of eyes at Hugh. He was in an attic room, pacing back and forth. Falcon watched as another man with a taser in hand came into the room and motioned for Hugh to move out.

Falcon moved his attention to the birds around the house, landing with several of them on the walls around the garden. Cawing loudly, they told him they'd keep watch.

Chapter Five

Hugh

Later that evening, Hugh led the way into the maisonette he was renting. His head had begun hurting once more and Imogen had suggested they head back there. He saw the surprise on both Falcon's and Francis's faces as to how close they were to the shopping arcade, where their shops were. He thumped up the stairs, too tired to care much.

"Make yourselves at home." He gestured to the sofas as they entered the living room.

"Bloody hell!" Falcon exploded. "Talk about having a front seat!"

Hugh grinned for the first time that day. He watched as Falcon and Francis began examining the scope he had set up overlooking the arcade.

"I'm going to get a shower," he declared. "Imogen can show you where the kitchen is if you want a drink. I'll be out in a few."

Hugh made his way to his bathroom, where he stripped and climbed into the tub with the overhead shower. He much preferred his own walk-in shower back in Manchester, but needs must. He groaned as the water flowed over him. He still ached a bit from being mis-handled when the goons had thrust him into the Land Rover, and he was still a bit sore after being hit with the heavy duty taser that Bentley had used on him earlier that day.

He arched into the spray, enjoying the hot water. After a few minutes he stepped out and grabbed a towel from the heated towel rack and dried off. Pulling the towel round his waist, he left for the bedroom.

Falcon Byrde leaned against the doorway to the room, grinning at him, his eyes ranging over him from head to toe. In his hands he held a small green first aid kit.

"I don't need that," Hugh asserted.

"Let me be the judge of that," Falcon said as he advanced on Hugh. His hands brushed against Hugh's left shoulder, where a graze had bloomed.

"Really…" Hugh faltered as he felt the other man's hands on him. "I'm fine."

"Let me just clean this and any others up." Falcon smiled at him, his hands gliding down to Hugh's sternum to where the taser had hit him. A deep bruise was already beginning to form.

Hugh sucked in his breath as Falcon got some arnica from the first aid kit and smoothed it onto his chest. He tingled all over, not just where Falcon had touched him, as he felt the beginnings of arousal.

"He got you well and good." Falcon frowned.

"It was a heavy duty taser," Hugh agreed. "Bastard enjoyed himself."

A moment later, Falcon stood back and smiled. "Best I can do." He then surprised Hugh by leaning in and giving him a small, sweet kiss on the lips. "Get dressed, we need to make some plans."

Hugh watched as Falcon left the room, his fingers going to his lips. He smiled, shook himself and quickly grabbed clothes from his dresser.

#

Falcon and Francis had taken the large scope to pieces whilst he'd been in the shower. It was piled in its component parts against the wall near the large French Doors overlooking the arcade.

Falcon looked pleased with himself as Hugh moved over to see what they'd done to his prized possession. Everything appeared to be in order. Then with an evil glint in his eye, he turned to them.

"There's a tiny camera in your bookshop." He laughed at the look on Falcon's face. "Only the one, I couldn't get into your back area."

Falcon grunted. "I expect you'll be taking it down now?"

"Of course."

"Guys!" Imogen butted in. "Less of the macho bullshit. We need to try and figure out what's going on."

They laughed, Imogen's words breaking the tension that had crept into the room. "I've contact Gil Summers," Imogen said as she took a seat on the sofa. "He's worked directly with Robert several times, and out of all of us probably knows him the best. He was aware of Ian but had never met him. He said he had a couple of things to tie up from his last job, then he'll head to York."

Hugh nodded. He had a lot of respect for the older agent. He stood up and began pacing.

"What I still don't understand is Ian's involvement in the Goodkind case. The family were involved in County Lines drug smuggling, but they weren't in charge. When I was there, I was gathering information for the agency to pass on to CID and to find out whether there was any need to pass it to MI5. The Goodkinds were at the bottom of the pile."

"Was there anything else that they may have been involved in?" Falcon asked. "Anything that would have brought them to Ian's attention?"

Hugh shook his head. He couldn't think of anything that stood out. "Maybe Gil will have an idea. All I know is that they were working out of an old shop in the high street in Peterborough. I paid them a visit, but couldn't get anything out of Old Man Goodkind, so I left my card with him. The next I heard was that the whole place had gone sky high. I understand you were there that day?"

Falcon looked up at him and met his eyes. "Obviously I survived," he deadpanned.

"How sure are we that the bomb was meant for the Goodkind family?" Francis asked from where he was leant against the French doors.

"What are you implying, Dad?"

Imogen had gone white as she turned to Falcon. "If, as Hugh says, Ian wants you dead…" She broke off.

Falcon looked at his father. "You can't…"

Francis hugged his son. "It was a close call. You told me yourself that if it had gone off only a few moments earlier then you would have been caught up in the blast.

Hugh felt an unexpected tug of pain in his heart then. He might never have met this man if things had been different. He began to pace. He thought better when he was moving. After a few circuits of the room, he realised he was getting nowhere. He shook his head.

"Let's shelve that for now. Maybe it was a coincidence,

maybe not, but there's nothing we can do about it now."

"Except look out for ourselves even more," Falcon said.

Hugh grimaced. "Ian was very insistent that I kill you. Why? What have you done to upset him?"

"Specifically? I don't know. I'd never heard of him until now. Dad?"

Francis returned his son's look. "It might pertain to the job John McKenzie has set us. He was at university with Robert and Ian."

"That's some coincidence," Falcon replied.

"Is that the priest you met with the other day?" Hugh asked, frowning. "What's he got to do with anything? Imogen had him checked out, he's squeaky clean."

"He is, you're right." Francis smiled. "Then maybe it has something to do with why John reached out to Falcon in the first place."

Hugh arched his eyebrow in question and looked at Falcon who returned his gaze. Brown eyes met blue and Hugh could see the little crinkles around Falcon's eyes. "Want to share with the class?"

Falcon grinned. "What do you know about the Ninth Roman Legion?"

Falcon

Falcon could see the confusion in Hugh's eyes as he looked at him. As segues went, it was a bit of a doozy.

"Are you referring to the book I asked about the other day. Sutcliffe's?"

"Was there any specific reason you asked about it?"

"Yeah, I read it as a teenager. Wanted to revisit it whilst I was here, seemed appropriate at the time for reading matter.

But... how is it connected to what is happening now?"

"Falcon, stop prevaricating and bring him up to speed," Francis interjected with a sigh.

Falcon nodded, realising his fun at Hugh's expense was over. He could tease the man later.

"Father McKenzie approached me a few weeks ago. He had a token from Francis to confirm he was *bona fida* and he asked me that exact question – what did I know about the Ninth Legion? It seems that when he was a young priest working at the minster, he'd stumbled on some tunnels underground that appeared to have been forgotten about. His superiors at the time knew about them, and didn't want him pursuing it then. Being young and somewhat foolhardy, he began to investigate, but didn't have time to do a full exploration as he was transferred to a different posting.

"What he did find had intrigued him though. At the end of the tunnels was a warded room, with symbols on the door suggesting it was connected to the Ninth. When his duties brought him back to the Minster he decided to have another look." Falcon went on. "However, he's not able to get back down there now as his mobility isn't good. He asked if we could help. He knows that I run a Paranormal Investigative business here in York, so he reached out. He gave us details of several entrances, the one Falcon used was particularly tricky."

Hugh looked poleaxed. Falcon understood all too well how he was feeling. He'd had that look a few times himself when dealing with his father's investigations.

"You investigate paranormal happenings?" was the first question Hugh asked.

Francis nodded. "Have been doing so for over 50 years now. When I rescued the children and they began growing up, I brought them in to help me. It's made life a lot easier."

"Rescued the children?" he asked, though neither Francis nor Falcon answered him. "Does the government know? About the paranormal aspect I mean."

Falcon laughed and shook his head. "Technically, yes, but the less they know about details, the better. We deal with a lot of it ourselves. Haunted houses, demon summonings gone wrong, creatures from another dimension. We've dealt with it all at some point or another."

"All of it?" Imogen asked from where she sat next to Hugh. She had gone pale and was looking at them in a slightly confused manner. "I'm aware magic exists, but the rest of what you mentioned, that really exists too?"

Falcon nodded, watching Hugh as he did so. The other man looked as though he was thinking hard, then he shook himself, and muttered something under his breath that sounded like, "Well, that would explain that then."

He looked up at Falcon and his father. "Go on, what did you find in the tunnels? I know you must have gone in already." Then he paused and grinned. "Ah, that's how you damaged your ankle."

Falcon could feel his face going red at the remembered embarrassment. "Yes." He sighed. "I was too busy making sure Robin was okay, I didn't look out for my own feet.

Anyway, we didn't get too far that day, and I've not really had a chance to go back in again. Now that Francis is here, I was going to try again."

"I'll come with you," Hugh said, straightening up. "You'll need some backup in there, and no offence Francis, but you must be the same age as Father McKenzie if you were at school together."

Both Francis and Falcon laughed at that, though neither

explained why. "None taken, Hugh," Francis said. "Your offer is acceptable. I'd rather not send young Robin down there again."

He frowned at his son and Falcon grimaced. Yeah, it hadn't been his best decision.

"Could it be connected to the Ninth?" Hugh asked then. "I mean, that's a bit of a stretch, isn't it?"

"It is and it isn't," Falcon answered. "In the 1950s, a man name Harry Martindale saw what he swears were Roman soldiers marching along looking dishevelled and defeated. He was in the basement of the Treasurer's House at the time. That area and the Minster are built directly over where the Roman military base was, in the town of Eboracum. Which is why I'm inclined to at least check out what McKenzie saw."

"What I don't get is why he left it so long to investigate again. Why didn't he let someone know what he'd found?"

"I was away a lot at the time." Francis replied. "It's likely he couldn't get hold of me, and he wouldn't have wanted to just let anyone know. Then when he became involved in his new career, it slipped to the back of his mind. I guess his relocation to York Minster brought it back to his memory and he contacted Falcon upon Francis's recommendation.

"Could Ian know about this in any way?" Imogen asked thoughtfully.

"I really don't know," Francis said. "Though why he'd be interested is beyond–"

"Okay," Falcon interrupted. "McKenzie has arranged for me to visit the Treasurer's House after closing. I suggest Hugh comes with me. We'll see what we can see there before going further into the tunnels under the Minster."

"I agree," Hugh replied.

Falcon could see that the other man was intrigued, he'd perked up when they'd mentioned paranormal happenings.

"You've had some experience?" he asked.

"A little." The other man answered.

"Well." Imogen stood up and stretched. "I don't know about anyone else, but I'm tired. It's been a stressful few days so I'm off to bed. I've taken the spare room, Hugh. Gentleman, I'll say goodnight."

She made her way to the doorway, before turning round again. "Oh, and there's no way I'll be going into any tunnels. I'll be backup and provide information when I can, but tunnels? No."

Falcon grinned at her as she left the room. He'd quickly come to like Imogen and realised why Hugh was such good friends with her.

"We can't forget Ian is out there," Hugh said with a frown. "I'm coming to the Treasurer's House too and we should try and make sure no-one goes anywhere alone."

Francis and Falcon agreed.

After a few more moments, having agreed to meet up with Hugh the next day, they left for the shop. As they entered Stonegate Alley, Francis looked up to where he knew the French doors were in the maisonette they'd just left. Hugh was still there, looking out. He raised a hand when he saw them and Falcon felt him watching them as they entered the shop.

Falcon had a warm feeling as he felt Hugh's regard. It felt safe having the other man watching over him. He looked forward to getting to know him better.

Chapter Six

Hugh

Hugh watched and waited until he saw Falcon and Francis enter the bookshop and lock the door. He stayed a few more minutes at the window, watching the arcade down below, then turning round, he began to re-build his scope. He'd feel better with it available to watch over the Byrde men.

As he finished, he felt a presence behind him and turned around to find that Imogen was watching him. She was now dressed in pyjamas, obviously ready for bed.

"What?" he asked.

Smiling, she walked over to him and tucked herself up under his left arm.

"I like him," she stated.

"Want to know a secret?" he asked, grinning at her. "So do I."

"I can tell, I think he likes you as well."

Moving together, they entered the kitchen and Hugh put the kettle on, whilst Imogen got some tea out – chamomile since it was late at night and they both needed to sleep.

Hugh stretched. He could still feel his bruises, but after Falcon's ministrations earlier, they felt better.

As he waited for the kettle to boil, he thought over what they had learned that evening. Try as he might, he still couldn't bring together Ian Swales and his need for Falcon Byrde to be killed. He shuddered at the thought.

"I've heard from Gil," Imogen said as Hugh poured hot water into their mugs. "He'll be here in a couple of days. I didn't mention anything about the tunnels or the Ninth Legion, I think that's something he needs to hear from us when he gets here."

"Did he mention anything about either Ian or Robert Swales?"

"No but I also contacted Peter in the office. I asked him to keep it quiet and see if he could find anything out about Ian."

"That's a good idea. Peter's a great analyst and researcher. We need to find out where Ian could have stashed Robert. And what about the place where Ian was supposed to be being kept securely?"

"I'll get Gil to put out some feelers when we see him. I did a quick google search, and the place where Ian was originally sent to was shut down about six months ago. The residents were all sent to different secure hospitals after that. There's nothing about Ian himself online at all."

Hugh sipped his tea, then blew on it as it was still a bit hot. Imogen put her hands around her mug and sipped slowly.

"Why don't you go to bed, Imogen? You're falling asleep at the table."

She smiled at him and taking her mug with her, headed off to the spare bedroom.

Wandering into the lounge, taking his mug too, Hugh

checked the large scope once more, then set the night vision camera attached to it to record. He checked the flat, making sure doors and windows were closed and locked before setting the alarm.

Yawning, he entered his own room and began to get undressed. He looked at the doorway where Falcon had been earlier and smiled as he remembered the glint in Fal's eyes while he was looking at him. He was really looking forward to getting to know the other man better and seeing where this feeling he had would take them.

Grinning, he finished his tea and got into bed. There was lots to do tomorrow, and he needed his sleep.

#

After a quick breakfast, Hugh and Imogen headed round to Falcon's bookshop. Hugh waved at Ella in the café as they went by. He'd stop and introduce her to Imogen later.

"Hi, Abbie," he greeted the teenager, who was once again on the till. "Is your boss in?"

Abbie grinned and nodded. "He said to give you this when you got here."

She held her hand out. On it was the little camera he'd installed in the shop a few days ago. He accepted it with a smile of his own. "Fal!" Abbie shouted. "Your guests are here."

An indistinct acknowledgment came from the back of the shop and moments later the man himself appeared. He was dressed in form fitting black jeans with a pale blue dress shirt. Hugh couldn't take his eyes off him.

"Good morning," he greeted them. "Hey, Abbie, this is Imogen Lovell and you already know Hugh McHughes.

They're going to be working on a project with me and Dad for a while. You okay to hold the front of shop?"

"I'm fine, Fal. Rachel is due in today for a shift," she replied, mentioning their other assistant. "So we should be covered. You go do your mysterious stuff!"

Hugh grinned as Falcon led them through to the back of the shop and into his personal space. He gestured for them to enter the room to their right and they found themselves in a well-presented study. Francis was already in there sitting at a small conference table.

"Come in, come in," Francis said, getting up and shaking their hands. "No problems this morning?"

"No, everything is fine today," Hugh replied, taking the seat indicated. Imogen pulled up a chair beside him and they both helped themselves to the carafe of coffee after a gesture from Falcon.

Hugh held the camera out and grinned at Falcon. "Thanks for retrieving this for me. Sure you don't want to leave it in place? Could prove useful."

Falcon grinned back and shrugged. "No need. I'm having my brother Ollie come in and fix us up with a new security system. We have external cameras, of course, but I thought I'd follow your example and fit some internal ones as well. At least this way my staff will be aware of them."

"Ollie?" Imogen asked. "Is that short for Oliver?"

"No. His given name is Oleander. Don't ask. He hates it."

Imogen only nodded and turned to Hugh. She poked him and he grunted. "Bring them up to date."

Quickly, Hugh summarised the information Imogen had found out the previous evening.

"So we've no way of knowing what happened to Ian after the home he was in was shut down?" Francis asked. "Seems a bit strange as it was a private secure hospital and not local authority funded."

"All I could find online was that the owners decided to close it down. There was no mention of who the inmates were, of course, just that they'd been relocated. Strange thing is that on their blog for a couple of weeks before this announcement, they were saying how well their expansion was going."

"Sounds dodgy," Falcon agreed.

"What's on the agenda for today?" Hugh asked.

"I thought we'd take Father McKenzie up on his offer to meet Myrna the National Trust manager at the Treasurer's House and go and look at the cellars. You still okay coming with?"

"Sounds good," Hugh replied. Not only was he intrigued about what had happened in those cellars over 60 years ago, but he would get to spend some time with Falcon.

"Whilst you're doing that, I'm having coffee with John – Father McKenzie that is," Francis said. "I want to catch him up about Robert and Ian and warn him to be on the lookout for anything strange."

"What about you, Imogen?" Falcon asked.

"I'm going to set up in the flat here and organise the 'back office'. I'll liaise with Peter, our analyst back in Manchester"

"Be careful." Hugh said. "I'll be glad when Gil's here to offer more backup." "I'll be careful." she replied. "It's not my first rodeo."

"Do you have Myrna's contact details?" Hugh asked Falcon.

"I do. I'll call her in a few moments and work out a time to meet with her."

"Okay." Francis stood up. "I'm off to meet John. Take care

all and keep in touch."

#

Falcon

Falcon arranged with Myrna to meet her at lunchtime. There were no tours of the cellars booked in that day and she was happy for them to see the area. She sounded intrigued by what he told her over the phone and was looking forward to meeting them.

Walking over to the Treasurer's House through York's historic streets was a lesson in history, Falcon always thought. They weren't far from the Minster and still within the area of Roman Eboracum.

Falcon and Hugh dropped into an easy pace, as though they'd been walking together for years.

"What's your take on the idea of it actually being connected to *the* Ninth Legion under those tunnels?" Hugh asked him.

"Sceptical," Falcon replied easily. "I'm not convinced. Until I see what's down there myself it's hard to speculate."

"And McKenzie said no-one else is aware of them now. Doesn't that seem unlikely?"

"I asked him about that, and he just shrugged and said many things had changed since the 60s. The people who knew about it when he was young man appeared not to have passed that knowledge on."

"Yeah, that I don't understand. Maybe your father will get more information out of him, seeing as they've been friends for years."

"I hope so," Falcon agreed as they crossed to Chapter

House Lane and the entrance to the Treasurer's House. Gaining entry through the main door, Falcon led the way to the ticket sales.

"Hi," he greeted the man on duty. "We're here to see Myrna Booth, she's expecting us."

"Yes, sir. I was told as much. Just a moment and I'll call her down."

Falcon and Hugh waited as the man contacted Myrna on the walkie talkie hanging from his belt.

"She'll just be a moment," the man said before turning his attention to the middle-aged couple who had come in behind them.

They moved away slightly as they waited. Falcon looked around. It had been many a year since he'd been in the Treasurer's House, though it never changed.

Something about its previous owner Frank Green insisting it stayed the same as he'd had it when he transferred it to the National Trust.

"Gentlemen." The voice came from a petite, dark-haired woman as she approached them. "I'm Myrna Booth, welcome to the Treasurer's House."

"Thank you," Falcon replied, introducing himself then Hugh. "Father McKenzie speaks highly of your father," she said to Falcon.

"Yes," he replied. "I believe they were at school together. In fact, they were meeting for coffee this morning to catch up."

Myrna smiled. "This way, please. Father McKenzie said you were interested in seeing the cellar where Harry Martindale saw the Roman Soldiers in the 50s?"

"We are." Falcon agreed. "He is following up a project and asked us to help out." Myrna led them down to the cellars and unlocked the door.

"How much do you know about what Martindale saw?" she asked them.

"I've read a couple of interviews with him and seen him being interviewed on TV. He was always adamant about what he witnessed. Very believable."

"He was," she replied. "I was lucky enough to meet him when I was a lot younger, I was volunteering here when I was at university, and they came in with a TV crew to do some filming. From what I heard and saw, he certainly believed what he had seen was completely true."

"Here we are." She entered the cellar where Martindale had been working. It was rather dark and they had to rely on a feeble overhead light. Falcon switched his phone light on to augment the light coming from overhead. There wasn't much to see. A stone wall and cellar floor, both devoid of markings. He shone his torch along the wall where it met the floor then out to capture more of the area.

"He was over here on a ladder when he saw the first Roman soldier." Myrna moved to stand where Martindale's ladder had been, facing them. "The Roman soldiers appeared in front of him, about where you are Mr McHughes, then marched in a straight line towards the wall over there."

Falcon and Hugh turned to follow the direction she was pointing in. "It's my belief the original Roman road to the barracks lies about 15 inches below the floor of the cellar?" Falcon asked.

"That's correct. If you follow it, it's a straight line to the fort which was situated about where the Minster is now. There are many Roman remains and treasures found when the Minster was built. Many of these are now on display in the undercroft."

"Our next port of call." Falcon smiled at her. He squinted,

trying to imagine what the young Harry Martindale had seen that had sent him into shock for two weeks. Into a lifelong belief that he had seen the soldiers. "He reported that the soldiers looked weary and unkempt. That they appeared to be disheartened. One of the things that stood out was his report that they were carrying round shields, different from the shape of the shields Roman soldiers normally carried."

Myrna nodded. "Years later historians discovered that about the period the Romans were in York, that they had experimented with using round shields for a short time. That wasn't known in the 1950s and gave verisimilitude to Martindale's tale."

Looking around the cellar, Falcon felt the atmosphere change. He glanced over at Hugh.

"Do you feel that?"

"I do," Hugh replied. "It's got distinctly colder."

Myrna looked at them in confusion. "Doesn't feel any different to me." Falcon stopped and closed his eyes. Reaching out with his inner eye, he was surprised to feel Hugh join him. He'd been unaware that the other man had any kind of psychic power. He opened his eyes to find Hugh looking at him with interest, as though he too had been surprised. The cellar still felt cold to him, and he could feel a strange disturbance.

Suddenly, his phone rang, shattering the quiet and the strange atmosphere. He swore, looking at the screen. It was his father.

"Dad?" he answered quickly.

"Fal, bring Hugh and come to the Minster library," Francis ordered.

"What's up?"

"Just come, quickly. John's missing." Falcon ended the call

and turned to Hugh.

"I heard," the other man said, already making his way out of the cellar.

"I'm sorry, Myrna, we'll have to cut this short. We need to go and see my father."

Myrna could only nod. She led them back up through the main hall. Saying goodbye and promising to keep in touch, they made their way out into the sunshine. Fortunately, they didn't have far to go.

Falcon squinted against the sun, looking at the strange sight of police cars with flashing lights outside the library of the York Minster.

Chapter Seven

Hugh

Hugh followed Falcon across the park to the library. His mind was reeling from finding out that Falcon had psychic powers as well. He rarely used his but had thought in a case like today's that they could come in useful. Imogen tried to encourage him to use them more, but he only did when he thought he wouldn't be detected. Which is why he'd been surprised about Falcon.

"What's going on?" Falcon was saying now. "Dad was going to meet John for coffee at the café. I wonder what he's doing at the library?"

"We'll soon find out," Hugh replied as he saw Francis waiting outside the library for them.

"Dad," Falcon greeted his father. "What can you tell us?"

"Come." Francis indicated that the two men should follow him inside the library.

They went downstairs into the archives where there were lockers and a reading room. A couple of police officers were questioning staff and archives users.

Francis led them over to a large table, taking a seat so they could keep an eye on what was happening.

"John didn't turn up at the café," Francis began. "After I'd waited awhile, I tried his mobile number, but all I got was his voicemail. I then tried calling his PA. Joe confirmed that John had left to meet me and was as perplexed as I was. I began making my way over towards the Minster hoping there'd been no accident and that he was just delayed in some way. I even popped my head around the door of his office and Joe confirmed he'd not been back since I last called. However, Joe had rung around some of his colleagues and one of them, the librarian here, said she'd seen him only a few moments before.

"I quickly made my way over here." Francis continued. "Only to arrive to find the place in an uproar."

He indicated to the people the police were talking to. "The archivist over there is Phillipa, she was helping the man they're talking to find an obscure reference in a book, when John burst in with a couple of men following him. She got up to see if she could help, but John just shook his head at her. He made his way to the section of the library where reference books were kept."

"What happened next?" Falcon asked.

"After he passed the book to the men with him, they grabbed him by his arm and started pulling him out of the library. Phillipa, bless her, stood in front of them and threatened to call the police. One of the men just sneered at her and showed her the taser he carried. He said if she interfered anymore, she'd be in trouble. John told her to move and allowed the men to pull him out of the library. Phillipa gave it a couple of moments then she and the person she'd been helping followed to see what was happening. By the time they got out the door, John was in a black car, which quickly drove off."

"Do we know what book?" Falcon asked his father.

Francis shook his head. "Not at the moment. I've not been able to speak to Phillipa without the police present to find out. When they've gone, I'll ask her."

"Sir?" One of the police officers had approached their table. Francis stood up.

"I'm Francis Byrde, a friend of Father John McKenzie. This is my son Falcon Byrde and our associate Hugh McHughes," he said.

When the policeman heard Hugh's name, his countenance changed, and his face lit up.

"Hugh!" he exclaimed leaning over to shake his hand. "Long time, no see. How are you involved in this?"

"Jack." Hugh grinned as he greeted the other man. "Gentlemen," he said, turning to Falcon and Francis, "this is Jack Speight. He and I went through basic training in the army together."

He turned back to Speight. "I'd forgotten you moved to York when you were discharged. How's Paul?"

"Great, great. Best thing I ever did was marry that man." He grinned at Hugh before his face went serious again. "What's your interest in Father McKenzie?"

"Francis here is a friend of Father McKenzie. I've never actually met the man. He and Francis were supposed to meet up at Stonegate Café, but to my understanding McKenzie didn't show. Francis tracked him here, just after he'd been taken away."

Speight turned to Francis, his notebook now in his hand. "Can you tell me what happened?"

Francis repeated what he had told Falcon and Hugh a few moments ago and Speight made notes, asking questions for clarification. Hugh couldn't believe their luck. Jack had been a good friend when they'd been in the army, and Hugh was sorry they hadn't kept in touch after they'd both left the forces.

"Thank you." Jack nodded at Francis then turned to Falcon and Hugh to find out what they knew. As it wasn't much more than what Francis had told them, it didn't take long to give their statements.

Phillipa had been hovering and came over when she saw that they were finished. She had a tablet in hand.

"Hello, Francis." She smiled at the older man. "It's good to see you again, even if it's not in the best of circumstances."

"It's not, Pippa," he agreed before introducing her to Falcon and Hugh.

I've checked the catalogue for what should be on that shelf against what's there. There's only one book missing: *A Picturesque History of Yorkshire* from 1899. Surprising really, especially as it's on the open shelves. Anyone can borrow it."

Hugh shook his head. "Sometimes that doesn't occur to people. They find it easier to just grab what they want."

"Any idea why that book?" Speight asked them.

No-one knew. Phillipa picked up another copy of the book from the open shelves to show them. Hugh looked through it before passing it to Falcon, but there was nothing in there that jumped out at him.

"I'll let Imogen know what's going on." Hugh stood up and headed for the exit, his phone in hand.

When he was outside the library, he rang Imogen and was happy when she picked up.

"Hey Hugh, how goes it?"

"Hi, Imogen. Not so good. Francis called us a half hour ago and told us that Father McKenzie was missing. He tracked him to the Minster library and found out that he'd been forced to take a book from the shelves, then he was forcibly taken away."

He heard Imogen's intake of breath. "That... that doesn't make sense."

"It doesn't," he agreed.

"Do we know what book it was?"

"We do. I was hoping if I sent you the details, you could have a look and see if there is anything you can find that might indicate why that book?"

"I'll do that," she answered. "Oh by the way, Gil's here. He made it earlier than he expected."

Hugh nodded and told her they'd be back soon he ended the call, before sending a text through with the full title of the book.

#

Falcon

Falcon and Francis joined Hugh outside the library. The shining sun made him squint for a few moments. He looked up at the sky and saw there were several birds flying around. He motioned to his father that he was going to sit on the nearby bench.

Falcon could hear Francis asking Hugh how his conversation with Imogen had gone as he leaned back, sending his consciousness out to join the birds flying above. It wasn't that he didn't want Hugh to know about his ability to connect with birds. After all, Hugh had his own powers, whatever they may be. He just wanted to tell him in his own time, not rushed as they were now.

As it was, he didn't expect to find anything out. Some of the birds here now may have been around when Father McKenzie was kidnapped, but not many.

As he suspected, he didn't get much. There were a few glimpses of McKenzie as he walked hurriedly with the other men towards to the library, then a couple as they left and got into a nearby car. Nothing after that. Hugh impressed McKenzie's likeness on some of the nearby birds and asked them to pass it on, much as he'd done when they'd been looking for Hugh. He just wished Ian, or whoever this was, would stop kidnapping his friends.

Francis and Hugh walked towards the bench.

"Let's go back to the shop. We'll order coffee and cakes at the café to tide us over until dinner," Francis said.

#

Falcon was pleased it wasn't far to his shop, nor that they met anyone he knew on the way. He was still slightly tethered to the birds, and as such not completely in the 'now' with Francis and Hugh. It took more effort than usual to put one step in front of the other.

Stopping at the café, they got coffee and cakes to take with them. Ella gave her uncle a concerned glance, then quickly got their order ready.

"Here," she said, passing everything over to them with an extra cup. "There's one for Abbie there too. She'll bitch if she gets left out."

Despite her words, she smiled when she mentioned her triplet. Falcon knew that although they argued like any other siblings, they were all very close. Hell, he and his own siblings had had some good rollicking arguments in their time.

Francis accepted the extra cup and thanked Ella, and she leaned over to give her grandfather a kiss on the cheek.

The men took their goodies back to the bookshop, and as they approached the door, they could see a courier was just leaving.

Falcon didn't think too much of it; he got books by courier all the time, Abbie would unpack them and add them to the database before putting them on the bookshelves. This time though, she was waiting for them biting her lower lip, looking anxious.

"Oh, good, you're back, Uncle Fal." She gratefully accepted her coffee from Francis before showing Falcon a small package. "This just arrived but it's addressed to granddad, so I didn't want to open it as usual."

Falcon examined the package. It was indeed addressed to Francis Byrde, c/o *Byrde's Books*. He handed it to his father, a frown on his face.

"Thank you, Abbie." Francis leaned in to give his granddaughter a hug. Then to the others he said, "Let's go into your study, Fal."

Falcon nodded and led the way to his study, which was just behind the mystery section. He pressed his palm against the electronic lock and entered when the door opened.

They settled around the coffee table, and Hugh made sure Falcon drank and ate something before they even began any discussions. Francis turned the package over and over in his hands. Falcon hadn't been able to see a return address when he had held it.

"You know who sent it?" he eventually asked his father.

"John." Francis replied. "It's his handwriting. By the looks of it, it was picked up by the courier this morning for immediate delivery."

"Are you going to open it?" Hugh asked, eying the brown package in Francis's hands.

Nodding, Francis got up and went to Falcon's desk across the room. He retrieved a small-bladed knife to open the package with. He pulled out a few sheaves of paper, turning them over and over in his hands, he looked at what he'd extracted. All he could see was what looked like a hand drawn map and a letter.

Francis held up the letter and read it out loud.

"My dear friend. By the time you get this, it may be too late for me. I'm sorry I dragged you and your family into this. Ian Swales has sent his goons for me, and I only have a few moments. Enclosed is a map of the tunnels I told Falcon about. Give him my apologies for involving him. Sorry, not making much sense. I have put an altered version of this map in a book in the library, which I will pass on to them to buy you some time. You need to find the room at the end of the tunnels. There are clues there and a… well, you'll find that out when you get there.

"I have to go. Goodbye old friend. John McKenzie"

"Wow." Falcon breathed out. "It sounds as though he doesn't expect to survive this."

Francis had his head down, rereading the letter from his old friend. He raised his wet eyes to meet his son's. "If it is Ian doing this, then you're probably right."

Falcon felt Hugh's hand on his back, as the other man rubbed between his shoulders, offering him comfort.

"What should we do?" he asked.

"I think we should visit the tunnels as quickly as we can," Falcon replied, already missing Hugh's hand, which he'd removed to pick up his coffee.

"I agree," Francis said. "The sooner the better. At least we know why that book is missing from the library now. We know he's put a false trail in there, but it won't take them long to work that out."

"Yes, but how does Ian know about it?"

"When John first mentioned this to me over 30 years ago, we were still in touch with Robert. John asked his opinion on the security aspect of it. Robert was an officer in the army at the time and was a security expert. Robert agreed John should follow his superiors' orders and not investigate it further. Ian was already in a secure unit under observation, but Robert was still close with him and visited him. Maybe he mentioned it to him? Though why, I don't know. Unless Ian had asked after John?"

"It's a bit difficult to speculate now," Falcon agreed. "Robert is missing and Ian's on the loose."

They sat in silence for a few moments, broken only by them drinking coffee and finishing their cakes. Falcon twitched the connection in his mind to the birds he'd sent searching for John, but nothing came back to him. He was worried. He was thankful to have found Hugh fairly quickly, but he didn't think he'd be so lucky this time.

"When shall we go?" Hugh broke the silence.

"This evening," Francis replied. He'd laid the map John had sent them on the coffee table, and they examined it as he spoke. It looks like the best entrance to use to access the tunnels is from the undercroft. It's usually closed by 5.30 pm, so we should be able to get in there after Evensong."

He held his hand out to show a small bunch of labelled keys, which had been in the package with the map and the letter. John had sent them a way in.

Chapter Eight

Hugh

Hugh returned to his maisonette in time for lunch and greeted Gil. Falcon had insisted on coming with him so no-one was out and about on their own if they could avoid it. Hugh brought both Gil and Imogen up to date on all they'd found out that day.

"I've no further news," Gil commented. "I'm still waiting to hear back from some of my contacts. No-one has heard from Robert in weeks. His wife isn't really concerned about him. She shrugged her shoulders when I visited her and just about said 'good riddance'."

"That's a bit harsh," Imogen mused. "I've met Virginia Swales a few times and she didn't strike me as the warmest of people, but even for her that's cold."

Hugh shrugged. He'd never met the woman, nor knew, or to be honest cared, about the Swales's marriage. Unless she had something to do with the disappearance of his boss, it didn't matter.

"What time are you headed to the Minster?" Gil asked

Hugh and Falcon.

"After Evensong, so about 6.30 pm. Want to make sure we're there before they lock up the Minster for the night."

"And how will you get back out again?"

"John sent Dad his keys." Falcon grinned. "He has a full set so we shouldn't have any problems."

"Even so, I think it will be best if I wait for you to return. I'll hide out in the undercroft and provide backup if it's needed." Gil was serious when he pinned Hugh with his glance.

Hugh only nodded. Having someone such as Gil as backup was comforting. He would certainly know what to do if anything went wrong.

"I'd come with Gil," Imogen said, "but someone needs to hold the fort down here."

Hugh grinned. Imogen was more of a backroom person than a get involved person, but he appreciated any backup she'd be able to provide.

#

The Minster was bathed in bright May sunshine, looking golden and regal in the early evening. Hugh and Falcon joined Evensong and would wander towards the undercroft once it had finished. Francis had gone straight down there so he could make sure the door was open and ready for them.

After the service ended, they slowly made their way over to the entrance to the undercroft, to join Francis. He was waiting with Gil, inspecting some of the Anglo Saxon carvings. The place was more open that Hugh had been expecting, but there was an area that was closed off with metal railings. Through that there was another door. Francis gestured them through it and closed it behind them.

"I'll wait here for you," Gil told Hugh. "This way I'll be out of view if anyone comes around."

Hugh nodded and agreed that was probably the best place for him. They'd spent their time well and had studied the map John had left them. There were three marked entrances on the map: the one Falcon and Robin had entered on their first foray, the one in the Minster and one from an old house on Ogilvy Street.

Both Francis and Gil were carrying backpacks, and Gil handed his over to Hugh. They contained spare torches, water, power bars and basic first aid supplies, which they hoped they wouldn't need.

Hugh slung the backpack over his shoulder and took one of the heavy-duty torches held out to him. He looked at the other two men, who were also carrying heavy- duty torches. Francis carried the map that John had provided them with.

Hugh was surprised how easy it was to find the entrance. Once they were through the fire door, there was a large open area, with piles of pieces of different types of columns and stone used in building the Minster. Using the information provided by John, they were able to find the entrance without any problems. He shone his torch around the entryway as they filed through. It was a fairly spacious foyer type area, where the walls had been finished and the ground was roughly paved.

"Interesting," Francis said as he looked around.

"Almost as though it used to be part of the Minster," Gil observed.

They spent a couple more moments looking around then Gil said he would stay there and wait for them. If there was a reason for him to leave, he would leave a message.

After a few more moments of discussion, Hugh, Falcon and Francis headed into the tunnel in front of them. Hugh hadn't realised how many tunnels there were as they traversed their way down the main one. They followed John's written instructions and the map and turned when they were told. Falcon had a piece of chalk, and he marked the turnings as they took them on the wall, numbering them as they went.

"This tunnel is certainly a lot more well-built than the ones Robin and I went down the other day."

Hugh looked around them as they went. So far, all the tunnels they'd turned down looked like they were uniform and had been dressed with brick. As they began moving further in though, they began to change, and the floor became more uneven. The walls were unhewn stone, that were devoid of brick or any other additions.

"Interesting," Hugh observed, still looking around as they traversed the tunnels. "Any idea how far in we are?"

Francis looked at the map. "Just under where St Leonard's Hospice used to be where Museum Gardens are now."

"We should meet up with the tunnels you and Robin used the other day soon," Francis said to his son as he looked around.

"Oh!" Falcon had stopped in front of them.

"What is it?" Hugh tried to see past him, but they'd entered a part of the tunnels where they were narrower.

"Dad, come and see this." Falcon stood aside, so his father could see what he was looking at.

"Ah. John's marker." Francis pointed to a spot on the map. They were getting closer to the area where Father McKenzie seen the Roman paraphernalia he'd mentioned to Falcon on his initial visit.

Hugh drew near the wall and saw a circle stamped into it,

with a bird in the centre and *Ordo Avian* written around it. He looked at Falcon questioningly.

"It's my sign," Francis explained. "The Order of the Byrdes. I set it up years ago. It's the sign – logo if you like – of our Paranormal Investigation Agency. John has a coin with it on. This is from him to let us know we're getting close."

Hugh nodded and followed the other two men as they went further down the tunnel.

They'd been under the ground for a good 15 minutes before they came upon the wooden door that John had told them about. The one he'd first seen over 40 years ago. Hugh joined the other two men and examined it.

There was no doorknob on it, just a hole from which a leather strap hung. It was so tempting to just reach out and pull the strap, but Hugh was always aware that there may be a trap.

"Thoughts?" Francis asked.

Hugh wasn't sure. He opened his inner eye and examined the door with his sight. The door glowed in his mind, and he could see there were a couple of spell traps. There was one on the leather strap and one on the door itself. He felt that Falcon was also examining it and he stepped back, pulling both the other men with him.

"It's booby trapped," he said, motioned them further back still. "I can see the spell traps, but I don't have the ability to do anything about them. My skills are limited."

"I was right," Falcon said. "I did feel you when we were in the Treasurer's House."

Hugh nodded. "I don't often say anything about my powers. They're fairly weak and a lot of people are uncomfortable whenever I show any kind of physic power. I've learned to keep it to myself, but I'm amongst fellow physics here."

"Yes," Falcon said simply. "I think you have an inkling what my power is?"

"You speak to the birds?"

"I do. That's how we found you."

"I thought it was something like that when those birds on the windowsill at the creepy house all moved their heads at once and looked at me."

Falcon laughed remembering that. "I have a little control over them and can use them as my eyes and ears."

Hugh nodded; his suspicions confirmed. He turned his mind back to the door. "There are two spell traps on the door. Not completely unexpected, but what is surprising is that they're new."

"How new?" Falcon asked, frowning.

"The one on the door is several years old. Decades, I think. Maybe from the time after John was down here? The one on the strap though..." He hesitated. "That's newer. Maybe a couple of years old. It's probably a good job you and Robin didn't get this far when you were down here before."

"A couple of years?" Falcon frowned. "That changes things."

"It certainly does," Francis added. "Who else knows about this?"

#

Falcon

Falcon stared at the door as though he could see what lay beyond it. "Well, what do we do now?"

"I'm not sure," Hugh replied.

Francis was also looking at the doorway in fascination. Falcon knew that anything like this was interesting to his father, but this didn't help them find what John had sent them here for.

"The map John gave you," he addressed his father. "Does it give any other ways into this part of the tunnel? We might need to come back and look at this further another time."

Francis got the papers out that John had sent to him and examined them. "He says in his notes that the three ways he indicates on the map are the safest ways in."

He squinted. "I'm not sure what he means by that."

"Perhaps there are ways he hasn't revealed on the 'false' map that was in the book that was stolen?" Hugh asked. "How strange is it that there are several ways in?"

"I'm not sure," Falcon replied absently. He was studying the map again. "I guess it depends on what it was used for?"

"That's the billion-dollar question." Francis replied. "Suggestions?"

"We need to find out what is protected behind that door," Falcon said, examining it once more as though it could have changed in the last few moments. "So, do we try the other route or go back and find someone who can help us remove these spell traps? And that's not to say there won't be others at the other entrance."

"Yeah, and who's to say when Ian, or whoever took the book, will be down here to try and get in from the other way?" said Hugh.

"They'll have to have good luck to get in that way," Francis replied. "From what John has sent me it looks like at least one of these entrances has been backfilled. If that's the one he's given them, then they may have to dig or blast their way in. And can you imagine what would happen if they tried blasting their way in – under York?"

Falcon smiled. It would cause an uproar. They'd have to dig, which would take time.

"Your friend is very sneaky." Hugh smiled at Francis.

"He can be, yes." Francis frowned. "I only hope he's okay."

Falcon shook his head. He'd check in with the birds he'd sent out chasing John and when they got back upstairs. He had to reinforce the impressions of John on them and send them out again.

"Maybe when we get back up to the surface," he replied to his father's unspoken question. He'd found before that he couldn't speak with the birds when he was underground. Unless they were as well. It was one of the limitations he had found.

"So." He looked at the other two after checking the time on his phone. "It's just after 9 pm. We told Gil to wait until 11 pm before worrying about us not returning. What shall we do, go on or go back?"

"Go on," Hugh replied immediately

"I agree," Francis added. "Let's try the other way in."

"We'll have to backtrack a bit first."

They turned around and using their torches to help them, they made their way back to the place where the other tunnel had branched off.

As they entered it, Falcon kept a wary eye on the floor. It appeared they were past the part where he'd twisted his ankle. He didn't remember going this far.

"Watch your head," came Hugh's voice from in front and Falcon noted that the ceiling had become noticeably lower.

They'd been walking for only a few more moments, when the roof above their heads got higher again and they came out into what appeared to be a hollowed-out atrium. They shone their torches around, but it was hard to get an idea of just how big the place was. They would need to come back down with arc lights if they really wanted to explore it properly.

Up ahead to their right was another dark opening, with a door inset about six feet inwards. Once again, they stopped and looked at the door from outside. Falcon turned to Hugh and could see he was using his inner eye to examine it.

"Well now, that's interesting," he said as he reached out to touch the door.

"Hugh!" Falcon shouted.

"It's okay," Hugh replied, stepping back again. "There were spell traps on this door. But they've been removed."

"What! When?"

"I'm not sure," he answered. "A while back? Sorry, it doesn't make sense. Why add one to the other door, yet remove one here?"

"Do you think it's safe to go on?"

"Not sure. Let's just take a breather before we go any further."

They all agreed and stood to one side. Falcon took his backpack off and got bottles of water for them all, passing them out along with power bars. They could all do with keeping hydrated and the sugar boost from the power bars would help them.

"If we do go on, we won't have too much time before we need to get back to Gil," Falcon said as he chewed on his bar. "I don't like the idea of him wondering what has happened to us."

"Agreed," Francis replied. "But having come this far, I feel we should at least see what's behind the door. It might not lead to the same place as the other one we stopped at, but the fact that someone has been here and removed the spell traps from this end is concerning."

"I vote we open the door, have a look and then get back to Gil," said Hugh. "We'll have to come back again anyway. I, for one, would like to see if we can find the filled-in tunnel that John gave details of on the 'false' map. See how hard it would be to get through and whether Swales is making any progress."

"I agree," Francis said, backing Hugh up.

"That makes three of us." Falcon put the now empty bottles and power bar wrappers in his backpack and slung it over his shoulder.

"Who wants the honour?" he asked, turning back to the door.

This one was a bit different from the other one – it was more modern, although still wooden, but this one had a proper handle.

Francis held out his hand and touched the handle. Nothing happened. Falcon held his breath as his father turned the handle and opened the door. It was anticlimactic. Again, nothing happened when he pushed the door open. It didn't even creak, just opened smoothly.

Falcon followed his father through the doorway, with Hugh bringing up the rear.

All three of them stopped and stared at what they saw.

"What… the hell!" Falcon breathed as he looked around him in astonishment. The room was set up like an old-fashioned gentleman's club, with a big desk to one side and comfy armchairs dotted around the room with low tables next to them. Along one wall was a long table with a decanter of what looked like brandy and several glasses. The other three walls were covered in bookshelves crammed with books. The floor was carpeted and there were several knick knacks around the room that could be associated with the Victorian era.

"Now this I was not expecting," Francis said as he stared. "This is nothing like John described to me. He did say there was an outer room before the one where he found the Roman artefacts, but not that it was set up like a gentleman's reading room."

"Never seen anything like it," Hugh agreed as he wandered off to investigate some of the books.

Over on the one wall that didn't have bookshelves, was another door. Falcon walked over to it and found himself with Hugh. His sudden companion put his hand on his shoulder and squeezed gently.

"Let me check it out first," he warned.

Falcon nodded and a moment later, Hugh did too.

"Same as the other one. There were spell traps on the outside, but again they've been removed."

"This just gets weirder," Francis said as he glanced at his smart phone for the time. "We need to be heading back soon."

"I agree," Hugh said. "Though I'm itching to open that door now. Just a peek?"

On the one hand, Falcon wanted to get back up top to try and get his head around what was down here. On the other, he also desperately needed to know what was on the other side of the door.

Francis was using his time wisely and panning the video camera on his phone around the room hollowed out from bedrock. His torch, which he'd laid on an ornate table, was his light source.

Taking a deep breath, Falcon pushed at the door. This time it was stuck. He got his shoulder to it and after a few hefty pushes and some grunts, he managed to get it moving.

Hugh was by his shoulder, one hand resting there. The warm touch was a comfort as he peeked into the room. At first, he couldn't see much of anything. Then as they both shone their torches around, he sucked in a breath.

"Damn!"

Chapter Nine

Malik

Malik was aware that there was something different around him. Some change in the air maybe? He wasn't awake, nor was he fully asleep. He floated in an in-between state that he hated. Nothing had changed. Nothing would change. Until now.

There was a noise that infiltrated through to his consciousness. This wasn't the first time he'd heard noises, but he was in no state to investigate their origin. If he was able, he would laugh at himself.

He lay there in the same state as always. Nothing made sense and he hated his inability to act.

The air shifted again, and whatever it was went away. He remained.

Chapter Ten

Hugh

Hugh gratefully took the cup of tea Imogen handed to him as they sat at the kitchen table in the rented maisonette. He took a few moments to enjoy the aroma of the Red Bush tea he liked, before setting it down beside his plate.

They'd got back late the night before from the Minster. Letting themselves out of the undercroft using John's keys, they sneaked out the side door, avoiding the cameras. No-one had said much on the way back to Stonegate. He and Gil had split off from the others after agreeing to meet later today at the bookshop.

Imogen had been up waiting for them, and after a quick rundown of what had happened in the tunnels, they'd all gone to bed. Now they sat eating breakfast, again ruminating on last night's activities.

"Any ideas who might have put the spell traps on the doors?" Gil asked, frowning. He'd taken Hugh's and the other men's possession of psychic powers in his stride. Imogen, of course, having known Hugh longer, already knew about his powers. She had been surprised to learn about Falcon though.

"No clue," Hugh answered Gil. "Falcon says he knows someone who may be able to help. He's going to contact them today and see if they're free to come and have a look with us. I'm more concerned about John at the moment. If it is Ian and his goons who've taken him, who knows what's happening."

Imogen reached out and put her hand on his arm. "Ian has a lot to answer for." Just then her phone rang, and she fished it out of her handbag.

"Peter," she answered, before leaving the kitchen to speak to their analyst from the office.

Hugh drank more of his tea. He wondered if Falcon had had time to reach out to the birds to see if he could find John. Somehow, he didn't think he would.

Imogen came back into the kitchen with a frown on her face. "I have to go back to Manchester."

"Is that safe?" he asked her.

"It'll have to be," she replied. "There's uproar over there. Robert's wife Virginia has finally put in a missing person's report for him and the police have been granted a warrant to search the offices. Someone needs to be there to oversee what's happening. They also need to know about Ian. I'm not sure Virginia knows her brother-in-law has been imitating her husband."

"I'll come with you," Gil said standing up. "Unless you think you need me here?" he asked Hugh.

"No. I'd feel better knowing you're with Imogen across in Manchester. See what's happening. If you can though, I'd like it if you both came back here tonight or tomorrow? We don't know when we might have to go back into the tunnels again."

"I can go on my own…" Imogen protested. "No." Hugh and Gil both said at the same time.

Imogen hmpfed, then began clearing the table quickly, whipping Hugh's tea away before he'd even finished drinking it. He watched her as like a whirlwind, she dumped everything in the sink before grabbing her bag and keys and looking at Gil in irritation.

"Well, come on then if you're coming. There's a train in half an hour."

Gil sprang into action and grabbed his jacket before joining her at the door. "I'll text you when we get there," he said to Hugh.

"Look after her."

Gil nodded, then followed Imogen.

Hugh sat at the kitchen table in the now empty room. He got up and flicked the kettle back on. Reaching for his mug, he put another teabag in it and made himself a fresh brew. He wondered why Virginia had gone from not caring what was happening with her husband, or where he was, to reporting him missing.

Seeing the time on the kitchen clock, he swore. He was going to be late at this rate. Taking his tea with him, he headed for his room to finish getting ready for the day.

#

Being a Saturday, the bookshop was extra busy when he arrived, and all Abbie could do was wave at him and gesture to the back. Taking that as a sign he should go on through, he headed to Falcon's study and knocked on the door before entering.

Falcon and his father were sitting on the comfy sofas. Both

looked rested after their adventures the night before and looked up and smiled at him.

"On your own? I thought Gil and Imogen were coming with you?" Falcon asked. "They were, but Imogen's had to go back to Manchester and Gil's gone with her to be on the safe side. Robert's wife Virginia has finally reported her husband missing and the police want to search the offices and question the staff. As manager, Imogen felt she had to be on site."

"That doesn't sound like Virginia," Francis answered, frowning. "There must be something or someone who's prodded her, as she wouldn't have done this on her own. So long as the money's still coming in, she couldn't care less about Robert or what's happened to him."

"That's a bit cynical, Dad. Even for you." Falcon frowned.

"Sorry. Maybe uncalled for, son. But that woman has always rubbed me up the wrong way."

Hugh took the seat on the sofa next to Falcon and felt the other man's heat all along his left side where they met. Soon, he'd have to see about getting Falcon to himself and exploring what was happening between them. Their attraction was definitely mutual.

"Any news"? Hugh asked.

Falcon shook his head, his eyes hooded as he turned to look at him. "I've searched as far as I can using the birds' eyes and unlike when you went missing, there's no sign of him."

He sighed. He'd really hoped Falcon would have been able to find John so they would be able to get him back. There were too many questions about what was happening in the tunnels, and Hugh was sure he'd been holding out on them.

"I have, however, spoken to my friends," Falcon went on. "Percy will come along with one of his partners Andrew on

Tuesday to have a look at the spell traps. They can't come any earlier due to other commitments, but Percy was interested in the photos I sent him and will work with his coterie to help find a solution for us."

"Coterie? You mean like a coven?" asked Hugh.

Falcon laughed. "Something like that."

Before he could go on, there was a knock on his door and Abbie put her head around it.

"So sorry to interrupt, Uncle Fal, but there's a policeman here says he needs to talk to you."

"It's okay, Abbie." He sighed. "Why don't you show him in."

Abbie nodded, then opened the door wide to show Jack Speight, the policeman who had been at the library after John's disappearance.

"Jack." Hugh got up to shake the other man's hand. Falcon gestured for him to have a seat. He took a chair next to Francis, his eyes taking them all in.

"I'm sorry I don't have any good news," he began. "Father John McKenzie's body was pulled from the River Foss early this morning."

Francis gasped and put his head in his hands. The others sighed; they'd been expecting the news in one way or another.

"I'm sorry for your loss." Jack turned to Francis. "I know you two were old friends."

"How did he die?" Hugh asked. "Did he drown?"

"No." Jack grimaced. "He was already dead when he went in the water. His throat had been cut and he bled out. Our coroner thinks he'd been in the water for several hours before he was found. He was probably killed not long after he was taken."

* * *

#

Falcon

They were quiet after Jack Speight left, all of them with their own thoughts. Though it had been expected, they were still saddened by the unnecessary death of John McKenzie. As soon as they found out who it was, Falcon didn't expect them to survive long.

Finally pulling himself out of his spiraling thoughts, he looked across at his father. Francis was pale and he reached across and squeezed his shoulder.

"Alright, Dad?"

Francis looked up before addressing his son. "I'll admit I'm shaken by this. It seems…" He broke off and shook his head.

Getting up, Falcon went over to the desk in the corner. He opened the bottom drawer and pulled out an almost full bottle of whiskey. If anything called for a tot, this news did. He filled three glasses and brought them back to where the others were seated. Francis took his thankfully and sipped it carefully with his eyes closed.

"Any news from Imogen?" Falcon turned to Hugh and handed him his glass. "Nothing yet," Hugh replied. "But they'll not have been in Manchester that long.

I'm sure she'll contact us when she knows more."

"Did you know Virginia, Robert's wife, well?" Hugh asked Francis. "I never met her. She never came to the office, not even for any of the social dos."

"She always was high maintenance," Francis replied. "We could never understand why Robert married her. It wasn't as though they were in love, and he certainly didn't need her money."

"Who knows why some people get married," Falcon replied absently.

The news of John's death had completely derailed them. It was as though all the interest in what was happening had been sucked out of the room and they were floundering.

"Does John have any family?" Falcon asked his father.

"Not anymore. His wife died a few years ago and he was an only child, so no siblings." He stretched and stood up. "I'm going to wander down to his office and offer my assistance to his PA Joe, in getting the funeral sorted. I'm sure they'll have it all organised but… I need to be doing something."

"What do we do now?" Hugh asked after Francis had left.

"There's not much we can do until after the weekend." Falcon replied. "As much as I'd love to go back in the tunnel and try and find out more about what was happening in that inner room, I realise we need to be better prepared."

"We could do some research and try and find out who was responsible for that room. I can't believe someone hewed out that area underground for a gentleman's library. And that inner room…"

Falcon broke off as he remembered the one view he'd got of the room before they'd returned to the surface. It was a room full of weapons. There were swords, spathas from the Roman army, katanas, foils, broadswords, hook swords. Every type of sword you could think of was represented. On one of the other walls there were different types of guns, from the original flintlock through to a gatling gun. There was nothing more modern than the nineteenth century though, which was another question to be answered.

But it had been the sarcophagus in the middle of the room that had made them stop and wonder. It was black marble, highly polished, with an opaque top. A quick look inside had left them with more questions than answers.

"Something is tickling at the back of my mind about that marble sarcophagus," Hugh said to Falcon as he helped himself to coffee from the jug on the table.

"Any clues?"

"Nope, it was something I read, but where or when I couldn't tell you."

Falcon nodded. He knew what it was like when something tickled the back of your mind like that, and it was usually better to leave it until it coalesced than try and force it.

Hugh's phone rang and he answered it immediately. "Imogen," he said. "Hang on a moment. Falcon's here, I'm putting you on speaker. Okay, go ahead."

"Falcon," Imogen's voice came through the speaker. "Gil and I are at the office in Manchester and honestly, it's a mess. Sometime between Peter phoning me and Gil and I arriving, someone has been into the office and trashed it."

"Is Peter okay?" Hugh asked after his colleague.

"He's fine. Fortunately for him he'd gone to get coffee and something to eat whilst he waited for us to arrive. He got back just after we got here and was gobsmacked at the state of the place."

"Have the police been?"

"They're here now. The Detective Inspector in charge is an old friend of yours Hugh, Deidre Matlock. She's confirmed that they're investigating Robert's disappearance, and it was her who we were supposed to meet when we got here. Obviously, she's now looking into this break in as well. Hugh, she'd like to talk to you at some point. She has your number and will probably phone you sometime today. Anyway, just wanted to bring you up to date."

"Is there anything missing, Imogen?" Hugh asked.

Falcon kept an eye on him. He was looking more stressed than he had been earlier that morning. It was one thing after another, and Falcon made the decision that they needed a break.

"I'm not sure yet," Imogen replied to Hugh's question. "Peter and I are going through everything, and I'll get back to you when I know more."

"Okay, give Deidre – DI Matlock – Officer Jack Speight's name. I'll text you his number. He's the one we've been talking to here about Father McKenzie. Oh, oh shit! Sorry Imogen, almost forgot to let you know. Jack called here earlier this morning to let us know that John's body had been found in the River Foss. He was already dead before he went in the water."

"Damn!" Imogen replied. "It gets worse. I'll let her know. You all okay?"

"Francis has gone to see if he can help, and Falcon and I are doing a little research to see what we can find out about that room."

"Okay, be there in a moment." Imogen's voice was further away. "Sorry about that. I have to go. I'll phone you later."

"Take care, Imogen. Keep us updated." "Will do."

"Let's have a break," Falcon said, smiling. "I'd love to take you out for dinner and have a proper date, see if this thing between us can go anywhere."

Hugh looked at him, and for the first time that morning, a small smile was playing around his mouth. "You've felt it too?"

"Definitely. You're a good-looking man Hugh, and I'm definitely attracted to you." Falcon grinned.

"Then," Hugh began as he got up and pulled Falcon up

with him, until they were standing facing each other, "let's see where this goes…"

Falcon put his hands on Hugh's hips and pulled the other man to him until their bodies were touching. Bending slightly so he could reach his lips, Falcon pressed a gentle kiss upon them.

Hugh opened his mouth, welcoming him in, and Falcon set out to explore. God, he tasted good. They stood like that for a few moments, kissing and exploring each other's mouths, before breaking away to take deep breaths. They grinned at each other.

"Well, dinner?" Falcon asked again. Hugh nodded.

Chapter Eleven

Hugh

He and Falcon had heard nothing new from anyone during the rest of the day and Hugh returned back to his place to get ready for their date that night. He was looking forward to getting to know Falcon better, having been attracted to him right from their first meeting.

He showered and shaved before carefully choosing an outfit. Dressed in dark wash denim jeans paired with a jewel green Henley long sleeved shirt, he pulled a lightweight jacket on before jogging down the stairs to the outer door.

Falcon was waiting for him on the street and Hugh checked him out as he was being checked out in turn. His date was wearing a pair of crisp chinos and a dark blue t-shirt. Hugh smiled at him and they fell into an easy step as they began walking towards St Helen's Square in the Georgian heart of York.

"Thai okay?" Falcon asked.

"Yeah, love Thai."

They crossed the square, passed the famous *Betty's Tea*

Rooms, now closed, and headed towards the grand Mansion House, turning left as they approached. Ahead of them was a small Thai restaurant.

"This okay?"

"Looks great."

Falcon opened the door, allowing Hugh to enter first, before following him into the small restaurant. It was still early, so there weren't too many diners yet.

"Falcon." A small Thai woman approached them, smiling widely. "Good to see you again."

"You too, Pom. This is Hugh, my date. Hugh, Pom," he introduced.

"You want sit in the window?" Pom asked Hugh as she gathered a couple of menus.

"Sure," Hugh replied, making his way over to the four-seater table in the corner near the large window. Falcon took the menus from Pom. After ordering a couple of Singha beers, they began perusing the menu.

"What's good?" Hugh asked.

"Anything, really, though I'm a big fan of Pad Thai myself. Depends on how spicy you like it."

Hugh looked at him, one eyebrow raised. Falcon just laughed before returning to his menu.

Pom arrived back with their drinks and they both ordered the sharing platter to start followed by Pad Thai. Once they were left alone a comfortable silence fell over the table and Hugh found himself people watching through the large picture window.

"How long have you lived in York?" he asked Falcon, turning back to his dinner companion.

"Ever since Francis rescued us, so about twenty years now."

"Rescued you?" Hugh asked, hoping Falcon would respond this time.

Falcon cocked his head to one side, reminding Hugh of the birds that had sat on the windowsill of the bedroom he'd been held captive in.

"You don't know? It never came up in your research?"

Hugh shook his head. "All the info I had said you and your brothers had been fostered by Francis Byrde before he adopted you, and that you all remained close. So much so that you and the others rented the shops in the arcade together. I didn't see anything about any rescue."

Falcon sat back in his chair, just as Pom approached with their starters. "Okay?" she asked.

"We're fine, Pom, thanks for asking."

She nodded and left the starters with them. Distracted for a moment by the food, the two of them filled up their plates and began sampling the offerings.

"You know I can connect psychically with birds, use their eyes as if they were my own and even communicate with them?"

Hugh nodded, wondering where Falcon was going with this. "My own powers are a lot less than that," he answered. "As you saw the other day, I can sometimes get feelings about what has happened in a room and occasionally I get visions. Other than that, I can spot a spell trap a mile off, but it sounds as though you have a lot more powerful powers than I do."

"You could say that." Falcon sighed and drank his beer. "When I was a child, I was held in a facility for children with psychic powers. We were all orphans and had been signed over to the facility. I was 7 or 8 when I first went there. They… they experimented on us with drugs…"

He trailed of, and Hugh reached over to grab his hand, hardly believing what he was hearing.

"On children?" he asked, horrified.

Falcon nodded. "There were six of us when I first went there. The rest were older than me and then others came in, including those who became my brothers and sisters. Some of the older ones never came back. I can't say for sure, but I think they died due to the experiments being carried out. They were trying to understand our powers and used drugs as a way to enhance them or block them, whichever way they wanted to go."

"That's..." Hugh trailed off, not sure what else to say. He squeezed Falcon's hand again in sympathy.

They paused talking once more and concentrated on eating for a while. Thoughts were swirling round in Hugh's mind. Who would do such a thing to children? It was bizarre.

"What happened?" he asked eventually.

"As we grew up, we were put on different drugs and our reactions were tested. In many ways we didn't question what was happening to us. We had no access to the outside world and thought that it was natural. That's just how the world was. Then Robin arrived and things got worse before they got better. He was only three when he came to the facility and he wouldn't stop crying for a long time. He didn't understand that his parents were gone, and this was now his home. They gave him a new drug and it affected him badly."

Falcon swallowed and Hugh could see the tears welling in the corner of his eyes. "You don't have to go on, Falcon, I don't want to push you."

"No, you should know. The drug they gave him did something to his circulatory system and he lost all feelings in his legs. Then he got sepsis." He took a sip of his beer.

"They had to remove his legs below his knees, that's why he has prosthetics now. A couple of years later, Francis came to visit the facility. He'd heard about it through his work with paranormal agencies and physic organisations and wanted to see what it was about. I think he originally thought it was a lot more beneficial than it was. He was horrified when he found out what was going on and used his influence with the government of the day to get the facility closed down. Robin and our baby sister Chyna were the youngest, I was 16 and Jenny was 17. We'd begun to dread what would happen when we got older as none of the older children had ever come back.

"Anyway, Francis rescued us, took us to his home in York and basically treated us as his children from then on out. It was a massive learning curve. TV, computers, smart phones, school – none of us had ever seen any of that, never mind had any contact with other children outside of the facility."

He fell silent again and Hugh kept hold of his hand, trying and failing to get his mind around what Falcon had told him.

Pom approached quietly and after tidying their starter dishes away, returned with their main courses. It broke the tension between them and Falcon smiled at him.

"It was a long time ago," he said as he dug into his meal. "Eat, Hugh."

Hugh nodded and they spent the rest of the meal talking about lighter subjects such as their likes and dislikes, including music, film and books. Both were great readers and found they had some favourite authors in common.

By the end of the meal the atmosphere between them was much more relaxed again and Hugh smiled at Falcon across the table. This gorgeous man with brown eyes that seemed to see into his soul, looked back at him and gave him a flirty grin. All thoughts of the heavier subject from earlier fled his mind.

"Are you ready to go?" Falcon asked, having paid the bill.

"Whenever you are."

They got up and after thanking Pom for the service, left the still fairly quiet restaurant heading towards Stonegate and the arcade.

"Nightcap at mine?" Falcon asked and Hugh agreed.

When they reached the bookshop, Falcon let them in then locked the door and reset the alarm. He led the way up the stairs and Hugh followed him into his flat. It was the first time he'd been in his home. The entrance opened up into a large, open-plan room, with a kitchen off to the left and several sofas spread around the area.

Falcon moved to a small bar in the corner and poured them both a glass of whiskey. Hugh found himself drawn to the wall opposite the windows where there hung lots of photos in frames. Many of them were of Falcon, his brothers and sisters and Francis.

He felt Falcon behind him and turned round to accept the drink.

"They date from when we moved out of the facility," Falcon said, pointing at one photo. In it, Falcon looked young and the others were crowded around him. He held a young boy in his arms. Robin, Hugh surmised. Jenny had a little dark-haired girl in her arms, and they were all squinting at the camera, not sure what was happening.

Other photos showed them more relaxed. There were wedding photos for Jenny and graduation photos for Robin and Ollie. There were even photos of them all grinning in front of the arcade shops, with workmen in the background.

Hugh leaned back slightly against Falcon, whose arms came round him as he began to kiss Hugh's neck. Hugh arched back, moaning at the feelings coursing through him, before turning in Falcon's arms.

They exchanged kisses, and as they became more passionate, Hugh held on to Falcon tightly. He could feel the other man's erect length pressed against his own and he drew in a breath.

"I want you," Falcon said as he nipped down his throat, before returning to his lips. "Bedroom?"

Hugh could only nod before he took Falcon's hand and let himself by led to the other man's bedroom.

#

Falcon

Falcon woke feeling sated and content. He could hardly believe his luck. Hugh was an amazing lover and so generous. He smiled as he watched him sleep in his arms and couldn't help himself as he pressed kisses to his forehead.

"Mmm." Hugh's voice was barely a whisper. "Good morning."

Hugh opened his eyes blearily. He smiled, scrunching his face at the sunlight coming in through the windows.

"What time is it?" he asked as he disentangled himself from Falcon's arms and sat up in bed.

"Just after 7.30 am."

Hugh yawned and stretched, showing off his muscles as he did so. Falcon watched appreciatively. They'd spent the rest of the weekend in bed, getting up only to eat and shower. It had been an intense time, and he could feel that he was already falling for the other man.

"Isn't today the day your friends are coming?"

"Yep, got a text from Percy last night. They'll be here by 9 am," confirmed Falcon. "Guess we better get up and get ready. Join me in the shower?"

Falcon grinned and bounced out of bed. Really Hugh had the best ideas. He entered the en-suite bathroom and got the shower running before taking care of business. Hugh joined him in the large walk-in shower. Falcon hadn't skimped when he'd fitted out his apartment. The shower was one of his luxuries.

"Hmm," he murmured as Hugh moved behind him and ran his hands down his body under the running water before reaching for the shower gel and pouring some on his hand. Falcon sighed as Hugh began to wash him, showing him great attention.

Falcon turned around and began soaping up the other man as well, returning the favour. He groaned as Hugh's hands reached his already erect cock and squeezed it. He thrust into the other man's soapy hand and moaned.

"That's it," Hugh said as he pumped him harder. "Give me all that you have."

Feeling his orgasm building, Falcon thrust harder, moving his hips back and forth. Not able to stop the sounds leaving his mouth, he let out a low groan as he came all over Hugh's hand and stomach. He let himself be held up by Hugh for a couple of minutes whilst he got his breath back then attacked his lips with a passionate kiss.

Returning the favour, he revelled in the feeling of the man in his arms.

Finally sated, they finished getting clean before shaving and dressing. Hugh had brought a bag over to the shop only the day before, so he had plenty of clothes and toiletries at Falcon's place.

#

Just after 9 am, Abbie led two men back to Falcon's study where he and Hugh were waiting for them. Falcon got up, a huge grin on his face, as he welcomed them both with a warm hug.

"Percy, Andrew," he murmured. "It's been too long. How's Pollie? The baby? The others?"

Percy laughed. "Everyone is fine." He grinned. "Baby Emma continues to grow and is a joy."

"Except at 3 am in the morning when it's your turn to get up to feed her," Andrew joked, extending his hand to Hugh. "Andrew Bryce, and this is Percy Smythe. At your service."

Falcon poured coffee for everyone as Hugh shook hands with the two men and they exchanged pleasantries. Once they were all sat around the room, Andrew looked at Falcon expectantly.

"What have you become embroiled in now?"

Falcon laughed. Nearly every time he met members of the coterie, he'd been involved in some investigation or other for his father. He'd have thought Francis would have been here this morning, but he'd sent his apologies. Falcon frowned slightly; he hadn't been able to find out what his father was up to, just that he was following up a couple of questions after John's death.

"Is everything okay?" Percy asked from where he was sat next to Andrew.

"Shall I?" Hugh asked Falcon and he nodded.

Hugh then told them why he'd been sent to York, about Ian

Swales taking over for his brother, who was still missing, and about his kidnapping. Falcon then joined in and between the two of them brought the coterie members up to date.

"Wow!" Andrew exclaimed. "When you fall into something you really fall."

"You could say that," Falcon agreed. "We'd love it if you two could come with us and look at the spell traps Hugh found. Though we can see them quite clearly, we don't have the skills to do anything about them. We're hoping you can help us untangle them."

"One of them is newer than the others," Hugh put in. "The other two feel as though they've been there for many years."

"I'm fascinated by this 'gentleman's club' type room you found under there," Andrew said. "I'm looking forward to seeing that."

"And what's in the other room. We only glimpsed in, not wanting to set off any other spell traps, but we saw a dark sarcophagus. No telling what..." Hugh swallowed. "... or who is in there."

"We need to find out who created the room as well. How does it connect to the Romans, specifically the Ninth. If it does at all. I'm not convinced on that."

"And the man who approached you – Father McKenzie. He's dead, you say?" "Yes, murdered. Francis is off following up some questions, but he hasn't shared anything with me yet."

"I hope he's okay," Andrew replied. "Your father has always been a great friend of ours."

"I'm sure he'll be fine," Falcon replied. "I probably worry too much."

He felt Hugh's fingers squeeze his as he leant across and kissed his cheek. "He'll be okay, Fal. As you said to me yesterday, he can look after himself."

All Falcon could do was nod, but he found it hard to ignore the jittery feeling in his stomach. He swallowed. He was sure something bad was going to happen soon.

"So," Percy began, "how do we get in these tunnels then?"

Chapter Twelve

Hugh

Hugh walked beside Falcon as they made their way to a part of York he didn't know that well. They walked closely, their hands occasionally touching, and at one point, Falcon wrapped his fingers around Hugh's and squeezed.

He grinned as they crossed Dean's Park, where a school party was in the process of demolishing their packed lunches. They weaved around the children who despite their teachers' attempts at order, were running around and playing. After walking past the Treasurer's House where Harry Martindale had seen the Roman ghosts, they turned into an old street called Ogleforth.

Hugh let out a whoosh of air as he saw the old medieval overhang houses on the right of the street.

"Wow!" he remarked. The others laughed at him.

"Just a bit further," Falcon said, holding his hand once more. "The building we're heading towards was once offices for people who worked at the Minster. It's recently been turned into accommodation, but it's a much older building that's been through several changes."

"And that's the entrance?" Andrew asked from behind them.

Hugh turned as Falcon did to address the other two. The road was narrow here and there wasn't room to walk four abreast.

"It's one of them," Falcon answered. "This one is in the old boiler room, which is in the basement of the building. I have a key."

He grinned as he held up the key and gestured for them to follow him through a wooden gate and round the back of the tall brick building. They then wended their way past parked cars and a couple of other buildings and down some steps. When they reached the door, Falcon opened it with his key.

Following behind, Hugh found himself in a fairly large room with machinery humming away to itself. Presumably the aforesaid boiler.

"This way." Falcon herded them towards the back of the room to another door, which opened with the same key. Behind this door was a flight of stairs and Hugh followed him down.

"Is this the route you came with Robin?" Hugh asked as they neared the bottom.

This was the second entrance to the tunnels he'd been in, and he was confused as to how many there were.

Falcon shook his head as he switched on the large torch he'd brought and gestured for the others to do the same.

Andrew followed behind Hugh and asked, "How deep are we?"

"At the moment," Hugh replied, "we're about 12 metres under the surface of York. The rooms we're heading to are about 15 metres."

Percy whistled. "As deep as that?"

"You have to remember that York's an ancient city and there have been several 'Yorks' built up over the ages. The Romans were only the first."

"Yeah," Percy replied as he looked around in the torchlight with fascination. They traversed through the tunnels for about 15 minutes until they came to an open area, and Hugh held up his hand to stop them going further. He swept his torch over the floor and drew in a startled breath. What he'd thought he'd seen in the gloom really was there. A body was lying perfectly still in the open area. He gasped as he realised he recognised him.

"What the fuck!" Falcon exploded as he joined Hugh, the others coming up to peer over their shoulders.

"I think he ran afoul of one of the spell traps Hugh told us about," Andrew said, stretching his neck trying to see further.

"I can't see any other spell traps," Hugh said as he moved forward. Percy agreed with him as they cautiously approached the body and knelt to examine it. Hugh put two fingers on his neck and sighed.

"Definitely dead," he announced before standing up and moving away. "I recognise him. He was one of Swales's goons that helped kidnap me a couple of weeks ago. His name was Parkin, I think. He was the one who tasered me."

Falcon reached over and rubbed his shoulder in sympathy at the remembered pain of the taser.

"Now what do we do?" Andrew asked. "We can't leave him here."

"No," Falcon agreed. "I'll sort something out. We can't let the police know where we found him, at least not yet. I'll get a couple of my brothers to move the body topside, and someone can 'find' it in the morning."

Hugh nodded. He couldn't think of anything else to do. It wasn't as though they could do anything for him now. He'd quite clearly died some time ago, maybe overnight?

Whilst Andrew, Percy and Falcon moved the body further towards the tunnel they'd come through, Hugh opened his inner eye and looked around the area, looking for more spell traps. There were none immediately visible and he examined the three tunnels that led off from the open area.

"Which one?" he asked Falcon when he came back.

"Falcon pointed to the one on the left. "That's the one that joins up with the tunnel that we followed from the Minster. That one in the middle is a dead end and the one on the right is the one that Parkin must have come down. It comes from under the Minster library. It was on John's map. The real one."

Hugh shook his head. There were far too many entrances to these tunnels than he was comfortable with. How no-one had stumbled on them in the last fifty years, he didn't know. Unless... maybe they had and had got caught out by the spell traps like Parkin. But then, he argued with himself, where were the bodies? He glanced at the tunnel on the right and wondered how easy it would be to block it up.

"How did he know it was there?" Andrew asked.

"When they took John, they got hold of a copy of the map of the tunnels," Falcon explained. "John had managed to fudge it, so it wasn't complete, and sent the original to Francis. Still, they must have been down here exploring. We have no way of knowing if there's anyone else down here or how much they've found."

"Let's hope he was the advance party and hadn't reported back to Ian yet," Hugh replied.

They made their way further along and Hugh realised they'd entered a part of the tunnels he recognized. Before too much longer they arrived at the door they'd found the other day that had the spell trap on the handle strap.

Hugh sighed in relief as he saw it was still there. Hopefully it meant no-one else had been this way.

He pointed out the tell-tale sparkles to Percy and Andrew, who both moved to examine them closer. After a few moments, they held hands, then both held up their free hands. Hugh saw a bright light come out from their hands and join together, which destroyed the spell trap.

Hugh let out his breath as the spell trap dissipated, leaving the handle strap free of any spells. They looked around the door and proceeded to knock the other spell trap out in a similar manner.

"That should do it," Andrew said. He leant across and kissed Percy, his paler face showing up in the torchlight.

"Who'd like the honours?" Hugh asked.

"I'll do it," Falcon said as he stepped forward. Hugh held his breath as Falcon pulled the strap towards him. Nothing happened.

"Hmm." Falcon examined the strap further. "Huh."

With a twist and a pull-push movement, the door opened a sliver. Falcon pushed and it opened a little more.

"Here," Hugh said, joining him at the door. Together they pushed and it opened even further. In the end it took all four of them to get it open and then they walked into an antechamber. It was dark and foreboding and smelled musty and deserted. It was also empty. Its stone-flagged floor was bare and the whole room felt cold and disquieting.

Hugh looked around carefully, shining his torch about the place. There was nothing else to see. It was empty. Another door loomed out of the darkness and Hugh immediately spotted the spell trap on it. Damn!

"Let's have a break," Falcon announced. Pulling his backpack from his shoulders, he handed out water bottles and some snacks. Hugh drank the water and inhaled his fruit bar quickly. The carbohydrates and sugar were welcome. As he ate and drank, he examined the spell trap, his forehead creased in confusion.

"I'm not sure this is of the same age as the others," he addressed Percy who was also examining the spell trap.

"I think you're right," he replied as he joined hands with Andrew. The sparkles in the spell trap brightened. "It's a bit older and laid down by someone different."

"Can you tell how old?" Falcon asked.

Percy shrugged, eyeing the spell trap again. "The ones of the outer door were of the 1960s. This one is older."

Andrew nodded, agreeing with Percy.

"It looks as though you were right, Hugh, and there's more than one layer of spell traps. Whoever used these tunnels and rooms weren't taking any chances on being discovered."

#

Falcon

Falcon swallowed the last of his water and screwed the cap back on. He placed it in the rubbish bag Andrew held out to him. He shoved his empty fruit bar wrapper in there as well. After everyone had finished, Andrew put the bag in his backpack to throw out later.

"How many entrances to these rooms are there?" Percy asked as he examined the spell trap again.

"I'm not sure," he answered. "We've been in the

'gentleman's club' room and the one that leads off that with that weird sarcophagus in it. Then this one. The map John sent to my father only showed the tunnels leading up to it, and one area which wasn't divided into rooms.

"Good job I brought these then," Andrew piped up, brandishing a sketch pad and some pencils. "Another time we can measure the size of the rooms, but for now let's just record them."

"Great idea." Hugh smiled at the other man. Falcon could see the crease between his eyes showing he was looking with his inner eye at the spell trap.

Percy's gaze focused inwards as he examined the spell. He reached for Andrew and Hugh and pulled them both into the connection. Falcon watched as the spell trap lit up and individual sparks flew from it as the three manipulated it.

After a couple of moments, the sparks merged together, and with a flash that made him jump, the spell burst from the wall and washed over them. He smelt smoke and ozone, before the spell dissipated in the air.

"Wow," Hugh said, losing the use of his legs and flopping onto the floor. Falcon moved towards him.

"You okay?"

"Just a bit overwhelmed. That's one of the largest workings I've been involved in. I'll be okay." He smiled up at Falcon. "Just give me a couple of moments to recover."

Falcon nodded and turned to Andrew and Percy, who were holding each other up. Percy nodded at him.

"It was difficult, but also old and had deteriorated. I was concerned it would go off before we could defuse it."

"Are there any others?" Falcon asked.

"Not here. Do you want to try the inner door?"

Falcon nodded, and Hugh reached up a hand for help to get

back on his feet. He wobbled a bit as he stood up and Falcon leaned in and planted a kiss on the other man's lips.

"Okay?"

"Better," Hugh agreed.

They crossed the flagstone floor to the other door. Not knowing where it led, Percy ran his fingers over it, checking it out with his inner eye.

"It's okay. Inert. Shall we?"

Hugh nodded and joined Percy. Lending his strength, they pushed. The door didn't move. They tried pulling, but again, nothing happened.

"Again," Falcon urged, and they pushed once more. This time something gave, but only a very small amount.

Hugh opened his backpack, and with a grin, brought out a long cable with a tiny camera on the end. He plugged it into his iPhone and then inserted the cable, camera first, into the small opening.

It didn't get far before it bumped into something dark. Hugh manoeuvered it so it went upwards, and after a short while, the camera showed a view of the sarcophagus room.

They all crowded around Hugh's phone and watched as the camera panned around, showing the wall where the door was. Paneling on the wall was stopping them from opening the door. The entrance between the two rooms had been effectively closed off.

"Now what?" Andrew asked.

"Are you okay to head around to the other tunnel and go in that way?" said Hugh. "Sure, we've got all day." Andrew replied.

Falcon agreed and led them around to the room he, Francis and Hugh had gone into the other day.

* * *

#

Opening the door at the other end, Falcon stepped back, letting Andrew and Percy get the whole experience of the 'gentleman's club' room.

He and Hugh watched as the other two men walked inside and looked around in surprise and wonder. Andrew gaped at the room, before turning back to them with a grimace. He looked pale.

"I know this room," he announced.

"What!" Falcon asked, looking at his friend.

"It's weird," Andrew said. "Familiar, but not. I've certainly never been here underground before. But this room is…"

"What?" Percy asked his partner, kissing his cheek.

"I think it's based on a different room," he mused as he wandered around before sitting in one of the large wingback chairs. "It's as though they reproduced a room I'm semi-familiar with here – underground."

Hugh looked confused. "Where did you see it? A museum?"

"No," Andrew replied. "In York in late 1874."

It was Hugh's turn to gape and Falcon drew in a breath. How had he forgotten that Andrew was not from their time?

"I'm sorry!" Hugh exclaimed, as he dropped into another of the large wingback chairs. A small cloud of dust flew up from the seat.

"I was born in 1849 in San Francisco in the States," Andrew began, smiling at Hugh's shock. "In 1872 I met Edward Harling. He was visiting San Francisco on behalf of his father who had business in the US. We fell in love."

He stopped and Percy leaned over to press his arm in sympathy, whispering soft words to him for a couple of moments. Andrew smiled then turned his attention back to Hugh.

"I accompanied Edward to New York where we found his father had died and he had to return to the UK. I decided to go with him. When we were in London, his sister Minnie got an invite to visit with Lady Emma Valois in Yorkshire. To cut a long story short, I became part of a magical coterie and was pulled through time to 2024 and Pollie's coterie."

"That's... amazing," Hugh replied. He looked at Falcon. "You knew?"

"Yes, I've known the guys a couple of years now."

"So you visited a club here in York like this?" Hugh asked.

Andrew shook his head. "Yes, near the Lendal Bridge." He laughed. "We were in there last summer on a family day out. It's a Pizza Express now."

Hugh joined in the laughter. "I've been in there. I didn't know it used to be a gentleman's club."

"It opened in 1869, so was only a few years old when I visited." He looked around him again.

"It's weird," Falcon agreed. "Do you have any idea of anyone you met back then who might have been involved?"

"I'll think on it," he said, pursing his lips.

"Right." Percy stood up. "Where's this mysterious sarcophagus?"

Chapter Thirteen

Malik

Malik floated towards consciousness again. His body was still in stasis, and he couldn't move. He could hear voices again. He strained to listen, but full consciousness was not within his reach.

He heard the outer door scrape open and wondered how long it had been since the last time someone had visited him. Time had no meaning here.

The voices came closer, and he could almost feel their presence. He could swear he semi-recognised one of the voices when someone declared, "Shit!"

Chapter Fourteen

Hugh

Hugh watched as Andrew reeled back from the sarcophagus and hid his face in Percy's neck. His lover held him, whispering to him and rubbing circles on his back. Percy looked at Hugh and motioned that they would be in the other room. He nodded.

"C'mon on, love." Percy led the shaken Andrew from the room and Hugh moved closer to Falcon.

"What happened?" he asked.

"Not sure..." Falcon leaned over and pointed out to him that the sarcophagus didn't appear to have changed from the last time they'd viewed it. Something had upset Andrew though.

Hugh followed Falcon in examining the sarcophagus and whistled. Made of black marble and coffin shaped, it looked as though it weighed a ton.

He opened his inner eye and as he did so, several sigils and engravings came into view. Some of them were written in Latin and one of larger engravings stated: *Hispana Nonus,* which translated as 'Spain Ninth'.

"The Ninth Legion." He pointed out to Falcon who had his hand on his shoulder so they could both see the engravings and sigils.

"I wonder if this is what Father McKenzie was talking about? And what does the Ninth Legion have to do with a black marble sarcophagus?" asked Falcon.

Hugh shrugged. He didn't have an answer. He only knew it referred to the Ninth, and it had been known as the Hispana legion, though they were not in fact from Spain.

"Guys!" Percy's voice called from the outer room, and they moved through to join them.

Looking slightly better, Andrew sat in the same wingback chair as earlier. He had a glass in hand and was sipping its contents slowly. Percy hovered over him, keeping a close eye on his lover.

"Are you okay?" Hugh asked as he leant against the library table nearest to where Andrew sat.

"I… I… will be." He gulped the last of what Hugh realised was brandy down in one mouthful. Looking at the table behind him, he could see where Percy had sourced the drink from. A large decanter stood there with its stopper secured.

"How was the brandy?" he asked out of curiosity.

The other man smiled at him; his first smile since he'd seen the sarcophagus. "It's surprisingly good, considering its age!"

He laughed with Andrew and it broke the tension that had been in the underground room.

Andrew sighed and took hold of Percy's hand, who squeezed his fingers in return. "I guess I should explain."

"Yes please," Hugh replied.

"When I was part of Lady Emma's coterie in Leconfield, I

met an Antiquarian called Gilead Summerbell. He was part of Lady Emma's social circle. She supported him in his quest to collect old documents and artefacts. He had quite the collection, including a 15th century gate which had stood at the entrance to Beverley Guildhall." He laughed.

"Gilead had bought it from them some years earlier and erected it in his back garden."

"Wow!" Hugh said. Fancy having something like that in your back garden. "What happened to it?"

"I think it was moved in the 1990s to outside the historic Friary in Beverley. Anyway, I digress." He paused, clearly gathering his thoughts.

"As I mentioned before, I visited the gentleman's club here in York with Edward and Thomas – another member of Emma's coterie. It was at Gilead's invite that we attended. He was an honorary member of the club as he visited the Philosophical Society in York many times and some of them were members at the club. To cut a long story short, he became mixed up with a secret society."

"*Hispana Nonus*?" Hugh asked. "Exactly! You saw the engraving?"

Hugh nodded and explained to Percy who hadn't been in the room about the connection to the Ninth Legion, then told them both about Father McKenzie's asseverations regarding the Ninth.

"And the sarcophagus?" Falcon asked.

Andrew closed his eyes as though remembering. "That was something else Gilead had in his garden at one point. There were many statuary pieces and other things there. I never saw it in situ, but he described it sufficiently to me that I recognised it."

"Where did that come from?"

"Beverley again, in the yard at the Minster there. Seemingly they were digging a grave and they dug up this marble tombstone shaped as a coffin. Of course, Gilead had to have it."

"How did he get involved with the *Hibernia Nonus*?" Hugh asked, fascinated by the story Andrew was telling them.

"He was blackmailed. Gilead was a homosexual in a world that didn't recognise homosexuality. He was caught with a local man by a member of the society. He thought he'd been set up. This man – I *think* his name was Jarratt – insisted Gilead help them search for various documents that had been lost for many decades, if not centuries.

"He was reluctant to tell us this, but he wanted to warn us to be careful. We were in a highly unusual relationship – one woman and five men. Society was already incredulous that Emma lived in the Hall with so many men, despite being married to Thomas. It gave them some privacy, but Gilead was worried about the rest of us."

Percy pulled Andrew towards him and kissed his forehead. Hugh also kissed Falcon on the lips. Once again, he was reminded of how lucky they were to live in the time they did when they could love who they wanted to, whoever they were and whatever their sexuality, without worrying about being arrested.

"Do you know what's inside the sarcophagus?" Hugh finally asked him.

"Not what." Andrew replied. "It's a who."

Hugh gaped at him. "There's a body in there?"

"No." Andrew replied. "If the spell they had Gilead find worked, then there'll be a sleeping vampire in there."

"What!" Falcon cried, and the room broke out into a hubbub as they all started talking at once.

"Vampires don't exist!" Hugh exclaimed. "They're myths!"

Falcon shook his head. "No, they're real."

Hugh turned to him, his mouth open in surprise. "You've met one?"

"So have you," Falcon replied with a slight grimace.

"What!?" He couldn't think he'd ever met any kind of creature of the night.

"Francis," Falcon said, reaching out to touch Hugh on the shoulder.

"Your father is a vampire? But… I've seen him out during daylight! He eats food!"

Hugh began to feel as though he was estranged from reality. Surely Falcon was jesting.

The other man nodded.

Andrew and Percy were quiet and Hugh realised he was the only one in the room who hadn't known that about Francis. He turned, taking the glass Andrew had been drinking out of earlier before rounding the library table. Unstopping the brandy decanter, he poured himself a generous slug and drank it down straight away. He slammed the glass on the table, the brandy burning on its way down. He coughed.

"Okay." He turned back to the others. "Say that I believe you. How do you know that's a vampire in there?"

He turned to Andrew as he asked the question. The other man joined him at the table.

"Gilead came to us one day in a fright. He'd been looking for this spell in many old documents for a long time and eventually he'd found it. He came to ask our advice, but all we could do was tell him not to share it with the *Hibernia Nonus*. We were going to meet with him later that week. We never got there. A couple of days after his visit, the chimera attacked the Hall, Edward died and I was dragged through time."

He was quiet for a moment. "I don't even know what happened to Gilead. I haven't thought about him since I arrived in this time."

#

Falcon

Falcon nursed his bottle of beer as he sat outside *The Judge's Lodging*. It wasn't too busy this early in the evening, but he knew later on it could get quite raucous. He'd waved Andrew and Percy off on the train back to Beverley and stopped here to try and work out what they should do next.

Hugh had returned to the maisonette as he'd had a call from Imogen and needed to sort something out with her about Swales's disappearance. He'd agreed to meet up with him later, but Falcon knew he was still shocked by his revelation about Francis.

"He said he was at school with John and the Swales twins?" he'd asked as they were walking back from Ogleforth.

"He did. What he didn't tell you is that he was wearing a glamour to make him look younger. He was investigating some of the strange goings on at the school and went as a pupil to fit in. His friendship with John was real though."

"Did he know?"

"Yes. I don't know how or when, but I think it's about the time he gave John the *Ordo* token."

Hugh had just shaken his head as he'd fielded a call from Jack Speight, letting his policeman friend know about

Swales's goon without giving away where they'd found him. Speight had said he'd get the force to find a magic user who could lift the spell trap from him. Falcon didn't hold out much hope of that happening.

His phone rang and he fished it out of his pocket. Francis's name appeared on his screen.

"Dad! Are you okay?"

"I'm fine, son. Sorry I was out of communication for a while. I've been helping sort out John's funeral."

Falcon could hear the sorrow in his father's voice. He knew he and John had been close, though he wished he'd shared more before sending him to talk about the tunnels. He knew Francis would have his own reasons for keeping information from him, but he still worried.

"You there, son?"

"I'm here. Can you come join me?"

"Where are you?"

"In the courtyard at *The Judge's Lodging*, nursing a beer."

"On your own?"

"For now. Hugh will be back later to join me. I need to update you on what's been happening."

"I'm at the shop. I'll be there in a couple of minutes. Order me a beer, will you?"

Falcon ended the call, caught the eye of one of the waitresses and ordered his father a beer, declining another one for himself.

The outside lights were coming on when he saw Francis enter through the open gates. He raised his beer in his direction and his father came over, dropping into one of the chairs around the table.

Francis took a sip of beer, before blowing out his breath in one long exhale. "It's been a hard couple of days," he acknowledged.

Falcon just nodded and sat with his dad, silently drinking for a few moments before Francis spoke again.

"Funeral's next week, in the Minster. It will be a full service. If you want to come, you'll be very welcome."

Falcon nodded again, but didn't add anything. He wasn't a fan of church services, but he could see himself joining his father to offer his support.

"Andrew and Percy came through today," he reported, before going on to tell him about what they had found, and Andrew's assertion that it was a vampire in the sarcophagus in the inner room.

"You've had a busy day! How did Hugh take it?"

"I'm not sure he believes me!"

Francis laughed. "He'll come around."

"Have you any idea who it might be?"

Francis shook his head. "I wasn't in York at that time. I was in Paris for most of the latter half of the 19th century. I only came to York in the 1930s. I didn't know about the gentleman's club Andrew mentioned."

Falcon looked up then and saw Hugh coming towards them. His step faltered as he noticed that Francis was with him, but Falcon grinned at him and Hugh returned the grin. He ordered from a passing waitress before joining them at their table.

"Hi." Hugh bent down and kissed Falcon on the cheek. He grinned and moved his head so he got his lips.

"Francis." Hugh acknowledged the other man.

"Hugh." Francis grinned. "I understand you had an interesting day today."

"You could say that."

Falcon watched as Hugh tried to unobtrusively examine

Francis. He could tell he was looking with his inner eye. He shook his head after a few moments.

"You really are a vampire," he declared in a whisper just after the waitress deposited his beer and left them alone.

Francis grinned again. "Guilty as charged."

"Is it rude to ask how old you are?"

Falcon laughed. That was always what everyone wanted to know, once they found out and accepted the truth of his being.

"I was born about 3,000 years ago."

"That's... amazing!" Hugh looked surprised but clearly interested in what had happened to him. "You must have seen so many interesting things."

Falcon knew if they got his father started on some of the stories from his life he'd not stop for hours.

"Hugh," he broke in before he could ask anything else. "How did your call go with Imogen?"

Hugh turned his attention back to Falcon and shrugged. "She's staying there for now. She and Gil are investigating what happened to Robert. It's being treated as a priority by the police and the powers that be. I think the idea that Ian, not Robert, had access to confidential documents for weeks is sending them crazy."

"Do they know about the tunnels and the rooms?"

"No. So far, we've managed to keep that just to those of us who have been there. After our discoveries today, the less people that know about this for now, the better."

Falcon and Francis agreed with him. It wouldn't do for it to come out that a sleeping vampire was been held in stasis under the streets of York. Whatever the *Hibernia Nonus* had been doing was a mystery.

"Had you heard of the *Hibernia Nonus* before?" Falcon asked his father.

Francis grimaced before shaking his head. "I don't remember anything about them, but as I was telling Fal earlier, I was in Paris at the time they were operating here. You have to remember, though, it wasn't unusual for secret societies to thrive in the upper echelons of society in the 18th and 19th centuries. You just have to look at the *Hellfire Club*."

"Weren't they involved in devil worship?" Falcon asked.

"There was no real proof that they were. Of course that wasn't the only club, the best known are *The Masons*, not that that was a particularly secret society."

They drank their beers, enjoying the mild May evening.

"In the meantime, we should investigate Gilead Summerbell and see what happened to him," Hugh said.

Falcon nodded as he finished his beer. Setting the bottle on the table, he stretched.

"Ready to call it a night?" Hugh asked.

"Yep. Dad?"

"I'll see you both tomorrow. I'm going to head home soon."

Falcon joined Hugh as he got up from the table. They said goodbye to Francis who remained to finish his drink. He was staring off into space.

"Is he okay?" Hugh asked.

"He'll be fine," Falcon said as he took Hugh's hand and began moving through the crowd out onto Lendal. People were beginning to spill out of the bar opposite now and the pavement and road were full. He manoeuvered them through towards Stonegate.

"You coming back with me?" he asked, pressing a kiss to his man's cheek.

"I think I can manage that!" Hugh laughed.

Falcon grinned and turned left through the alleyway to

the arcade. The outside lights were on and Falcon looked towards the shop and the figure waiting for him there.

"Hey, Raven!" He greeted his brother who'd been away for a few weeks. "Didn't know you were back."

"Just got back earlier tonight. We need to talk, Fal," he said while looking at Hugh. "You can talk in front of Hugh. We need to catch you up as well."

Chapter Fifteen

Malik

Malik nodded at the concierge as he opened the door to the York's gentleman's club. He entered and let the servant help him off with his coat and put it in the cloakroom.

"Good evening, sir." The major-domo said as Malik entered the main bar area. "Mr Jarratt and Mr Summerbell are upstairs in a private parlour and have asked that you join them when you arrive."

"Thank you, Simpkins," he replied, changing direction to head for the stairs to the second floor, and the smaller private rooms up there.

"Lord Malik." Gilead Summerbell stood to greet him as he entered. "Summerbell, Jarratt," he acknowledged both men, shaking their hands before joining them at the small table. He was confused as to why he had been invited to join them. He looked towards where Jarratt was holding up the whiskey bottle they were sharing. Malik nodded, and then accepted the drink he poured for him.

"Your health, gentlemen," he said, raising his glass and

taking a generous mouthful.

"I have to leave shortly," Summerbell stated. "I'm giving a talk to the Philosophical Society. Are either of you attending this evening?"

Jarratt shook his head. "Not this evening, Mr Summerbell. I'm afraid I have a conflicting appointment."

"I hope to drop in later," Malik added.

"Good." Summerbell nodded. Getting up, he shook both their hands again.

The other man's hand was sweaty, and Malik felt that he was shaking slightly. He looked at him, but he didn't meet his eyes. Before he could say anything, Summerbell quickly left the room.

"Well, Mr Jarratt, it's just the two of us. I presume you wished to speak to me about something?"

"I did indeed, Lord Malik. Or should I just say Malik. You're no more a Lord than I am!"

"I beg your pardon!" He wasn't staying here to be insulted. He tried to stand up but found he was unable to do so. Panic began to set in as he found that the harder he tried to move the worse it became He looked at Jarratt in horror. He tried to speak but couldn't.

The door opened and Simpkins and another man entered and came to stand either side of Malik's chair, putting their hands on his shoulders.

"Take him to the room underneath. I'll join you soon," said Jarratt.

Malik found himself being hauled up and manhandled between the two other men. He was slung over the younger man's shoulder and taken down the servants' stairs and through the kitchen. A heavy robe was thrown over him and he was thrown onto a hard surface, his head banging down on it heavily. Shortly thereafter they began to move. He assumed they were in some kind of vehicle.

His head throbbed and he felt sick. His usual healing wasn't working. What was it Jarratt had slipped into his drink? He faded in and out of consciousness, barely aware of the vehicle finally stopping. The men pulled him unceremoniously from it and dumped him on the ground. He heard hooves and wheels moving away and could feel the wet ground soaking through his clothes. The world seemed to have stopped moving and he was lost in a maelstrom of chaos.

#

He came to later to find he was sitting in a wingback chair in the main room of the gentleman's club. Where? What? His eyes darted around, taking in the familiar scene. But there were some major differences – no windows overlooking the river, and the ceiling was hewn out from bedrock. Most of the walls were covered in books and there was at least one door. Leading where, he had no idea.

He realised he was secured to the chair with ropes and still couldn't move. He squirmed as much as he could, trying to find any give in the ropes. He tried to remain calm and work out what he was doing there, but there were no clues in the room.

The door opened and Jarratt walked through. Ignoring Malik, he walked over to the table to one side of him and picked up a decanter. He poured himself a generous slug of its contents.

"I'd offer you one, but I don't think you'd drink it."

"You'd be right." He squirmed again. "Care to tell me what

this is all about?"

"I'd like you to know it's not personal," Jarratt said. "It's your nature that I require."

Malik looked at him in confusion. "My nature?"

"You are a vampire, are you not?"

He was surprised. How did Jarratt know this? Summerbell! It had to be. He'd stumbled on his secret a few years ago. Why had he let a stranger know? Realising that Jarratt was still waiting for a reply, he leaned forward as much as his restraints allowed, and looked Jarratt in the eyes.

"Yes," he said clearly. "Yes, I am."

Malik realised that whatever had been in the whiskey was not only stopping him from moving but was also preventing his vampire gifts from working.

"What is it to you that I am?" he asked.

Jarratt grinned. "I'd say I was sorry, but I'd be lying. I need your nature, your death energies as it were, to power a spell I need to cast. Unfortunately, there won't be much of you left at the end of it."

Malik stared at him in horror. He'd come across magic users who'd wanted to harness his death energies in the past, but none who'd actually had the means to do so. Spells that would allow them to carry this out were almost impossible to cast, let alone find.

"How?"

"I've been looking for a long time for a way to harness the energy you carry within yourself, that all vampires have within themselves."

Simpkins and the other man who had transported Malik here entered the room, then moved behind him. Before he could even think to struggle, his head was pulled backwards.

Simpkins roughly thrust a tube into his mouth, pouring some liquid down his throat.

He spluttered, trying not to swallow, and liquid poured from his mouth as he tried not to gag. Simpkins used his hands to stop him from spitting the tube out and keep his mouth closed. He had no choice but to swallow, else he'd drown. He thrashed about trying to dislodge the two other men.

Unable to help himself, he lost consciousness.

#

He floated between consciousness and unconsciousness as he lay naked on a cold flagstone floor. He wasn't able to open his eyes more than a slit. All he could see around him were pricks of light through the gloom. These eventually came into focus as lots of candles on the floor and on the walls. For some strange reason Jarratt was dressed like a Roman Centurian. He stood over him while Simpkins and several other men surrounded him. There was no sign of Summerbell.

Chanting began and Malik could just make out a Latin word here and there, though what he was hearing meant nothing to him. He was out of his depth and had no hope of rescue. As the chanting went on, he could feel his death energies being drained from him. As the lights around him wavered and went out, he screamed.

Chapter Sixteen

Hugh

Hugh sat beside Imogen's hospital bed, holding tightly to her left hand. His other hand was raking back and forth through his hair. He was barely holding it together. A phone call in the middle of the night was never welcome, but one telling him his best friend had been involved in a hit and run and was fighting for her life was definitely not on his to do list. Peter, their admin, was dead, having been killed in the same crash, and Gil was in another room of the hospital with a broken leg. He wiped his eyes and the moisture in them made his vision blurry.

The previous evening, Hugh had joined Falcon and his brother Raven in a quick meeting, where they'd swapped stories, and Raven had given them some food for thought. Afterwards, he and Fal had retired to bed. The phone call had awoken them at 2 am. Hugh had bombed it down the motorway to Manchester Royal Infirmary where Imogen and Gil had been taken.

* * *

#

"I'll come with you," Falcon had stated, grabbing jeans and a sweater. Hugh leant over and gave him a quick kiss

"You can't. You're working with Raven today, remember? You promised him."

"I'm sure he would understand," Falcon protested.

"I'm sure he would. But he needs your help today. Please, Falcon. Help your brother out, then come and join me. I..." He hesitated. "I'm not sure what I'll do if Imogen..."

He broke off and Falcon swept him into his arms. They were both still shocked at the news they'd just received, and Hugh soaked up the comfort he was being offered.

"I'll be okay," he assured him.

"I know you will." Falcon went over to the bowl beside the door in the living room. "Here, take my car. It's parked in St Mary's car park. It's a grey Vauxhall Meriva."

Hugh took the keys and memorized the registration number that Falcon rattled off. He hadn't brought his own car to York. Depending on how things went at the hospital, he might have to go and collect it from his flat in Manchester.

"Does she have any family?" Falcon asked as Hugh finished getting ready. "Yes, a sister Lucinda. She lives in Paris. I'll phone her once I have more news. They're twins, and I know she'll want to be here for her sister."

Falcon opened the door, then pulled Hugh in for a searing, possessive kiss. "I'll be there as soon as I can."

"I'll text you when I know more."

Falcon nodded and Hugh had run into the night, desperate to get to Imogen's side and find out what had happened to her and Gil.

* * *

#

Now sitting holding Imogen's hand, Hugh slumped over slightly in his chair. He was tired. They'd only got two hours sleep the night before. His phone buzzed with a text. He turned it over. Lucinda.

I'm at the airport. My flight leaves in half-an-hour. How is she?

He'd phoned her shortly after he'd got to the hospital, and she'd assured him she'd be on the first flight out.

Still unconscious.

See you in a few hours.

He texted confirmation and put his phone down again. The door to Imogen's room opened and he sat up quickly, his attention on who was entering

"No change?" DI Deidre Matlock came into the room and closed the door behind her. He shook his head. Matlock had met him at the hospital entrance to give him the rundown of what had happened. Imogen, Peter and Gil were en route to Peter's home to drop him off before returning to Imogen's for the night. They'd been driving down Princess Gate when a lorry had swerved at them and pushed them into the way of an oncoming tram. Gil, who had been driving, hadn't had a chance to pull out of its way before they were hit. The lorry driver had abandoned his cab and ran off towards St Peter's Square.

"No, she's still out of it," he replied. DI Matlock was one of the better DIs on the Manchester force; they'd worked together a couple of times a few years earlier when he'd been assigned as a consultant to her station. They'd gotten on quite well, so much so that he still got an annual Christmas card from her and her wife Pat.

"Gil's awake and asking to speak to you," she said as she took the seat on the other side of Imogen. "He's given his statement. I'll stay with her if you want to go speak to him."

He nodded and reluctantly got up, dropping a kiss on Imogen's forehead.

"Her sister Lucinda is coming in from Paris soon to be with her. Can you make sure your guys know?"

She agreed and Hugh left the room, nodding at the young police officer who was guarding the door.

"Sir," the man said in return.

He walked down the corridor to Gil's room and allowed the officer on duty there to hold the door open for him. He was pleased to see the precautions being taken. Gil was sitting up in bed waiting for him.

"Imogen?" he asked straightaway as Hugh approached his bed.

"Still out of it," Hugh replied. "She had surgery as soon as they brought her in, and the anaesthetic is still in her system."

Gil sighed and leaned back on his pillows. "Shit, what a night. I'm sorry, Hugh. I couldn't do anything."

"You did what you could."

"Peter still died though."

"He did, but you can't think of that, Gil. I've let his family know and they'll sort things out from their end. Your brother needs you to phone him when you're able to."

Gil's brother Adrien lived in Australia. Unlike Lucinda, he was unable to get there like he wanted.

"I'll phone him after this," Gil replied. "It came out of left field. I didn't even see the lorry until it was too late."

"Don't blame yourself, Gil. Nothing good ever comes of that."

Gil nodded and was silent for a bit. "I think we must have been getting too close to finding Robert. Ian probably panicked and sent someone to stop us."

Hugh agreed. DI Matlock had said something similar. They'd had a tip from one of the staff members, who had worked at the secure asylum where Ian had previously been held, to say that someone matching his description had been seen in another group home where the informant occasionally worked. Officers had gone to the home, only to find the 'resident' had recently been released. No other information was known about him.

"What's the damage?" Hugh asked Gil as he looked at the other man. He had a leg in plaster and his head and torso were bandaged.

"Lucky." Gil smiled for the first time since Hugh had entered the room. "Another few inches and I'd not have survived. As it was, I got away with a broken leg, cracked ribs, contusions down my right side and a slight concussion. I should be out of here in a day or so."

"I've arranged with DI Matlock for you and Imogen to be under protection whilst you're here. When you get out, you're coming back to York with me – you and Imogen both – where I can keep an eye on you."

"Now look here…" Gil bristled at Hugh's commanding tone.

"No. I mean it, Gil. You're a victim now and we need to keep you and Imogen alive. Matlock is going to liaise with the York police, and you'll be protected. Falcon's father has a house near the Minster that he's said you can use. It already has a stair lift installed from the previous tenant, so you'll be able to get up the stairs. I'll persuade Lucinda to come with Imogen when she's better…" he trailed off. *When. Definitely when.*

"Okay, okay," Gil conceded to Hugh's determination. "How are things in York?" Hugh spent the next hour bringing Gil up to date. He was as flabbergasted as Hugh had been about what – or who – was in the black sarcophagus. When Hugh told him about Francis, having earlier gotten Falcon's permission, Gil had been incredulous and didn't believe him at first.

"Shit. We leave you alone for a few days and look what happens!" he exclaimed.

Despite their lively conversation, Hugh could see that Gil was fading and suggested he rest. He was just getting up to leave when there was a knock at the door and the police officer peeked in.

"Miss Imogen is awake now, sir, if you wish to go see her."

"Thank you," he replied, waving goodbye to Gil and rushing back to Imogen's room.

#

Falcon

"Come through," Falcon told his brother as he and Hugh entered his study hand in hand.

Hugh sat in his usual place on one of the sofas and Falcon went over to the wet bar in the corner. He pulled out his best whiskey. He had a feeling they were going to need it. He poured three drams over ice before handing the glasses around and joining Hugh on the sofa. Raven sat opposite them in the wingback chair Francis preferred.

"Salut!" he toasted and sipped his whiskey. The others did the same.

"What do you need, Venn?" he asked, leaning back against Hugh's arm which was slung across the back of the sofa.

"Your help in confirming a sighting of Robert Swales." He dropped this tidbit into a pool of silence.

"You've found him?" Hugh asked, removing his arm from around Falcon and leaning towards Raven. "Where?"

"In the Dales. Nidderdale to be precise. Only thing is I'm not one hundred per cent sure. Which is why I need Fal to come with me and check."

"How–" Hugh started, before Falcon put his hand on his arm.

"Raven is named after the bird he shifts into," Falcon said, smiling at his younger brother. He remembered the young boy he had been and his shock and awe when he'd first transformed into a raven. Then the pain which had followed afterwards as the doctors at the facility tried to work out how he 'worked'.

"Wow!" was all Hugh said, looking at the other man in fascination.

Raven smirked. Falcon could see he was enjoying the other man's reaction. "Falcon can 'twin' with me when I'm in my raven form, see through my eyes, talk to me etc. I need him to be with me, to confirm my sighting, then we can let Francis know."

Hugh pulled his phone out of his pocket and brought up his contact for Robert Swales. The photo from last year's agency newsletter was attached to his details. He handed the phone to Raven.

"That photo's less than a year old. Is that who you saw?"

Raven squinted and looked at the picture. "I think so. I hesitate, only in that he doesn't look like that now. He's thin and looks undernourished. From what I could see his eyes were vacant. It's why I need a second opinion."

Hugh took his phone back and he replaced it in his pocket, yawning. Falcon finished his whiskey and put the glass down on the table in front of them.

"I'll see you in the morning," he told Raven. "If you come here for 8 am we can get a good start."

"Will do," Raven replied, getting up. "I'll drive us out a bit closer before I shift. Pateley Bridge isn't far from where I saw him, so we can find a quiet spot near there and seek him out."

Falcon agreed and after seeing his brother out, turned his attention to Hugh. "Ready for bed?"

"I am. Am I staying?"

Falcon leaned in and kissed him possessively, pulling him close until he could feel his erection pushing against Hugh's.

"Does that answer your question?"

Hugh's reply was to take his hand and drag him out of the study in the direction of the bedroom. Groping and kissing on their way, they fell onto the bed in a tangle of limbs.

#

Falcon was brought back into the moment by Raven's amusement. His mind was with Raven and his brother communicated through his brain that he'd rather not know what Falcon got up to in bed. He rested back in the car where he was sitting and answered that Raven should mind his own business. A cawing laugh was all he got in response.

#

* * *

Falcon soared above the moorlands, his ability allowing him to meld with his brother Raven as he flew northwards from their stopping point. He watched through Raven's eyes as he scanned the fields and buildings below him. Coming into view was a large, converted barn with seats and a hot tub outside. They were in Nidderdale, and he was nearing their destination – a holiday complex at Dallow Barns.

#

Raven landed on the roof of one of the buildings. All of them were holiday lets and only one of them appeared occupied. Raven hopped to the ground, investigating anything he found on the floor, but his eyes were on the open doorway, where a woman appeared leading what looked like an old man.

"Come on, Rob," she whispered. "Let's go and enjoy some sunshine. You know, like you were always promising me. 'We'll go next year, Ginny,' you always said, but next year never came. Your promises meant nothing, did they?"

The man cowered away from the woman as she pinched his arm between her fingers. He winced trying to move away, but he looked like he was drunk.

The woman, who Falcon knew to be Robert Swales's wife Virginia, known as Ginny, led him to a chair and forced him to sit down. He struggled a little, but not much. Now he looked as though he was drugged.

See if you can get a bit closer, he instructed his brother. Raven cawed and hopped closer to where Robert was sitting.

"Shoo. Shoo!" Virginia flapped her hands at him. Raven cawed in protest but hopped backward.

"Filthy bird." The woman spat at him. She sat next to

Robert and began nattering at him again.

"When Ian comes and sees you, he'll realise you're in good hands with me. We'll go away to France. You'll like it there. We can go Chateau hunting like we said we would when we were younger. Ian'll see that there's no need to get rid of you like he threatened. You can be with me. We can be as we were again..."

Falcon stopped listening to her ramble on about how they could be together properly for the first time in years. He felt sorry for her in a way, knowing she'd been neglected by her husband for a long time. But this wasn't the way to go about saving their marriage.

I've seen enough, he spoke into his brother's mind. *I'm going to step back now and phone Dad to let him know. See you back at the car.*

Raven cawed and lifted off into the sky once more. Falcon gently disengaged from his brother's mind and stared out of the car window.

He'd desperately wanted to go with Hugh this morning when he'd hared off to Manchester to be with Imogen. Hugh had argued that he needed to go with Raven if they were to find Robert and eventually, he'd agreed. He was glad he had now, as he could see that Robert was not in his right mind and needed medical treatment.

He pulled his phone out of the cup holder in Raven's car and thumbed it on. There was a new text from Hugh.

Imogen's awake, but in a lot of pain. Lucinda will be here soon, I'll let you know when she arrives. Any luck?

The text had come in half an hour ago. His fingers flying over the keys, Falcon replied quickly.

Found him, and his wife. Raven's on his way back. Going to phone Francis. Will meet you in Manchester later today.

I miss you. I'll send you my address so if I'm not at the hospital you can find me there.

After a couple more texts back and forwards, Falcon pressed the contact for Francis. He answered after a couple of rings.

"What news?" he immediately asked. Falcon and Raven had filled him in on their intentions over breakfast that morning.

"It's definitely him," Fal told his father. "Him and his wife. He's not in a good state though, Dad. The sooner someone can get to him the better."

"I'll inform the police and arrange to go there myself," Francis's voice came over the loudspeaker just as the car door opened and Raven slid into the driver's seat.

"Sooner rather than later," Raven said, getting comfortable. "He didn't look at well."

"I'll do it now then. Falcon, how are Hugh's friends?"

Falcon filled him in on what Hugh had told him about Imogen and Gil, before Francis finished the call to go contact the police.

"Can you drop me off at the nearest station where I can get a train to Manchester?" Falcon asked his brother.

"I can do you one better," he replied. "I'll drive you there."

"Thanks, bro," he replied, his mind already with Hugh as Raven pulled out of their parking spot and headed for the main road which would put them on the road to Manchester.

He looked up the journey on his iPhone and texted Hugh that he should be there within a couple of hours all being well. His reply came in straight away.

Good, see you then.

He switched off his phone and leaned back in his seat. "I'm going to see if I can catch a couple of hours of sleep."

Raven just nodded, his ear buds already in as he scanned the radio for a station to listen to. It wasn't long before Falcon fell asleep.

Chapter Seventeen

Hugh

Hugh quietly closed the door to Imogen's room behind him and turned towards the nurses' station. Talking to one of the doctors was Imogen's sister, Lucinda. Her hair, unlike her twin's, was in a cute pixie cut. Imogen preferred to wear hers in a chignon tied behind her neck.

"Luci!" He strode towards her, his arms held out.

"Hugh!" she cried and rushed into them, pulling him close and holding him tight. He could feel her tears on his cheek, and he reached into his pocket and removed a clean handkerchief, which he handed to her. She sniffed and wiped her eyes, giving him a watery smile.

"The doctor says she's making good progress."

"She woke up earlier, but only for a few moments, so that's a good sign." He turned her towards Imogen's room.

"Dickens," he addressed the PC on duty outside Imogen's door. "this is Ms Lucinda Lovell, she's Imogen's twin sister. Please show her every courtesy."

"Ms Lovell," Dickens replied as he opened the door for

them to enter.

Imogen hadn't moved and was still sleeping peacefully. Various IVs and other medical equipment were attached to her.

"She looks so small, lying there," Lucinda whispered.

"It's all the equipment," he agreed. Imogen wasn't a particularly small woman, but she was dwarfed by the medical equipment. He rounded the bed and took Imogen's left hand in his and sat down in the visitor's chair.

Lucinda stayed at the end of the bed for a while, before moving to sit in the chair usually reserved for the patient. She pulled it as close to the bed as she could.

"Can you tell me exactly what happened?"

Hugh nodded and repeated the information he'd been given by the police when he arrived. Lucinda's face showed her horror when he told her that Peter was dead.

She'd met him once when she'd visited them at work a couple of years ago. "Will you let me know when you hear about his funeral?"

"The family have already had his body collected by the funeral directors they're using. His brother promised to let me know when they had a date for the funeral."

"Have you had anything to eat?" he asked her as he stood up, leaning over to kiss Imogen's forehead.

"I had a sandwich on the plane, but I wouldn't mind a cup of coffee."

"I'll be back in a few moments then. They've got a Costa Coffee in the foyer, so at least it's decent."

Whilst he waited in line for the barista to make two takeaway coffees, Hugh checked his phone. There was a text from Falcon.

Hugh checked his watch. It was 4.30 pm. He'd been there

non-stop since 2am that morning. He would check on Imogen and Gil one more time before heading home. He fired off a text to Falcon with his address so Raven could drop him at his apartment building.

There was no immediate response. He watched the screen for a couple of moments, but no little dots appeared to say Falcon was replying to him. His name was called by the barista, so he collected the cups and headed back upstairs.

After handing a coffee to Luci, he headed towards Gil's room.

"You still here?" Gil asked, although he seemed pleased to see him. "Heading out soon. Falcon's meeting me at my flat."

Gil grinned. "You're smitten."

Hugh laughed; he couldn't deny it. He was smitten. Shit! He groaned. It was typical of him to fall for the guy he was originally sent to spy on. He grimaced.

"Have they given you an idea of when they'll discharge you yet?" he asked the other man.

Gil shook his head. "I'm hoping a couple of days. The doctors are of a different opinion."

Hugh grinned, like him, Gil didn't take well to inactivity. He hoped for his friend's sake it wasn't any longer than the few days he'd predicted earlier.

"Okay, I'll make sure you still have protection outside your door whilst you're here. Luci has arrived and is in with Imogen now."

"I'll go see them when they let me get up." Gil smiled and Hugh returned it, before saying he'd see him in the morning.

He checked his phone again to see a message from Falcon saying he was on his way and should be at his apartment block in about half an hour. It would take Hugh a bit longer to get there so he sent Fal the code to get into the building.

There were some sofas in the foyer he could wait for him on.

#

It took Hugh slightly longer than he had intended to get away from the hospital. Eventually though, about 5.30 pm, he set off. He'd let Fal know and asked him to pick up a takeaway from the Italian near his apartment block. He should be home soon.

He drove into the underground car park beneath his apartment block and parked Falcon's car in his visitor's space. It had been a while since he was home, and he dragged the basics he'd stopped at a Tesco Express for out of the boot. They'd need milk for their coffees, as well as breakfast stuff.

Closing the driver's door with his hip, he headed for the lift to take him to the foyer to collect Falcon.

He found him sitting half-asleep on one of the sofas, a take-out bag from the Italian on the floor next to him. Hugh leant over and squeezed his shoulder.

Falcon gave a bit of a start, then grinned when he saw Hugh. "Hey," Hugh whispered as he helped the other man to his feet. "Hey, yourself. How are Imogen and Gil?"

As he led Fal to the lift, he filled him in on how both were doing, mentioning that Gil would hopefully be discharged in a couple of days and Imogen maybe a week. He'd talked to Lucinda before he left, and she was determined to take her sister back to Paris with her when she was released.

"Probably for the best," Falcon agreed as they ascended to the 11th floor where Hugh's flat was.

"It will make it a bit easier for us. I can ask a friend to keep an eye on her. Pierre works for a sister agency in Paris and I'm sure he'll be willing to help. He owes me a couple of favours."

#

Falcon

Falcon yawned as he followed Hugh into his flat. He was shattered. Sharing with Raven when he was on one of his flights was always tiring. Hugh had taken the takeaway from him and preceded him into the kitchen.

Falcon looked out of the floor to ceiling windows and whistled. Manchester canal was laid out in front of them and there were a few lit up narrow boats going up and down. He stood there and watched them for a few moments, wondering who was on them and where they were going.

"Fal!" Hugh's voice sounded behind him, and he realised it was the second or third time he'd called his name.

"Sorry, just enjoying your view. It's brilliant."

"One of the reasons I bought the place. Not that I've had too much time to enjoy it up to now."

He nodded in acknowledgment, then began to help Hugh dish up the pasta and sauce he'd ordered from the Italian. He pulled out some garlic bread sticks and put them on the breakfast bar where Hugh had already put plates and glasses of beer.

"Have you lived here long?" Falcon asked as they ate.

"A couple of years. I bought it when I got the job at Swales's Agency. I bummed around different places before that. Lived in France for awhile. Stayed in Spain with my parents for a few months, but I missed the UK too much to stay."

"Are your parents still there?" he asked, this was the first time Hugh had mentioned his family.

"Yes, they retired there about ten years ago. Dad was CEO for a company in London, they were a big fabric suppliers. He retired when the company was sold. Mum enjoys spending his money!" He laughed, and Falcon could see his affection for his parents, despite his words.

The food was okay and after they'd finished, Falcon helped Hugh clear up before they headed to the living area with a second beer each. There were several photos displayed on an ornamental table near the window and Hugh took note of one of a gorgeous looking villa.

Reluctantly he moved away as Falcon's phone rang. "Hi, Dad, how goes it?" he asked Francis.

"We got them," he said, sounding tired. "Robert didn't even know who I was, he was completely out of it. Virginia was reluctant to let us know what drugs she'd been using on him, so we'll have to wait for the tox report."

"Did you find any clues as to Ian's whereabouts?"

"Nothing. Virginia isn't talking, though it's obvious she knows something and is involved in this up to her neck."

"Are you back in York?"

"Yeah, I'm at the hospital with Robert. I'll stay here for now. Is Hugh with you?"

"Yes, we're in Manchester. Gil's not too bad, but Imogen needed surgery. She's getting better, but still not awake for any period of time. Hold on, I'm putting you on speaker phone."

"Hugh?" Francis addressed him. "I'm sorry to hear about Imogen and the accident."

"Thanks, Francis. You found Robert then?"

"Yes, he's in hospital in York. I'm not sure if we'll ever get him back as he was. He's currently being assessed by psychiatric doctors. I'm sorry."

"Me too. I'll let the higher ups in MI6 know what's going on. I guess this is probably the end of my agency. There's a general call out to find Ian. The police have put a call out to the ports and the airports in case he tries to leave the country."

"I don't think he will. Whatever he's into at the moment, I don't think he's going to give up."

"No, I agree with you. What's happening with the rooms under York?"

They spent the next half an hour talking about what they should do next as regards the vampire they'd found in the black sarcophagus in the rooms underground. Several were suggested and discarded, in the end they agreed to let Francis investigate further before making their next move.

"Do you think Ian will attempt to enter the tunnels again?" Francis asked. "I wouldn't be surprised," Falcon replied. "I've tasked Ollie and Robin with keeping an eye on the entrances we're aware of. I've told them not to go down there but to let us know if they see anyone hanging around."

"I'm going to talk to someone I know at the Minster and get them to close off the entrance from the undercroft there. Even if they only put a temporary lock on the door, it will be one less entrance to worry about."

"What worries me," Hugh put in, "is whether there are any other tunnels we don't yet know about. I know we've got the map Father McKenzie left us, but how accurate that is we don't know. Nor do we know if he knew all the tunnels."

"When you will be back in York?" asked Francis.

"A few days at least," Hugh replied. "I want to make sure Imogen's going to be okay and see her off to Paris with Lucinda."

"I can come back earlier if you need me," Falcon added.

"No, you're okay, Fal. If I do need you, I'll let you know. I better let you go. I need to go check on Robert one more time and get home myself."

They finished the conversation and Falcon ended the call. His phone had only ten per cent battery left.

"Do you have a charging lead?" he asked Hugh.

"Check the second drawer on the right in the kitchen. It's my junk drawer."

Falcon grinned, didn't they all have a drawer like that, he rummaged through the it before he found what he was looking for. He plugged his phone in and left it on the counter.

"I don't know about you, but I'm ready for bed," said Hugh.

"Me too." Falcon picked up the small backpack he'd brought in with him. He'd quickly stopped and bought a few different things he'd need for staying over for a few days.

Hugh grinned at him. Leaning over the counter, he pressed a kiss to Falcon's lips.

"Let me show you where the bedroom is."

Chapter Eighteen

Hugh

Hugh ushered Falcon into the lobby of the building the agency's offices were located in. It was 11am on a Thursday morning and not too many people were around. A couple of security guards nodded at him as he led the way to the lifts.

"Are they on duty all the time?" Falcon asked Hugh.

"During working hours, there's always two on duty. After 6 pm there's one guy who patrols the building."

"Hmm." Falcon frowned as they entered the lift. "Has anyone asked what happened the night the offices were broken into?"

Hugh pressed the button for the 14th floor before he answered. "Jeff was on duty that night, but he was called away to investigate a fight in the back alley. There's a nightclub on the street over that way." He pointed behind them. "Jeff was in the alley for only a couple of minutes before he heard the disturbance and went to investigate."

"Convenient," Falcon muttered as they exited the lift.

"This way." Hugh placed his hand on Falcon's back and

motioned to the right. A sign on the door declared these to be the offices of the *Swales Agency*. Hugh put his hand on the metal plate next to the door and entered a code. The door slid open, and he gestured for his lover to precede him.

As they entered, they stopped and took in the mess that still covered the floor of the offices. The outer office looked as though a whirlwind had been through it and upset all the papers on desks. Drawers were pulled open, and laptops and computers had been smashed.

"I thought they'd begun tidying up?" Falcon commented as they made their way further into the room.

"They had," Hugh replied absently as he pulled out his mobile and pressed Gil's number.

"Gil speaking."

"Gil it's Hugh. Falcon and I are standing in the reception of the office, and it looks like it's still a complete mess. I thought you and the others had begun cleaning up?"

"We had," Gil's voice came over the speaker phone. "Can you put me on video?"

"Just a moment." Hugh played around with his phone and turned the video on.

"Wow!" Gil's sounded surprised as he looked at the mess through the mobile phone screen Hugh held up.

"Not what you were expecting?"

"No. Though there was a lot of mess originally, the laptops and computers weren't smashed and there's even more paper floating around now than there was."

Hugh looked around, taking it all in. Obviously there'd been another break in. He sighed. He'd have to contact the police again when he had finished speaking to Gil.

"Hugh," Gil spoke, getting his attention. "I'll send you a couple of pictures the crime scene people took the other day."

"Thanks Gil. I'll contact DI Matlock again and let her know."

They rang off, and Hugh dialled Deidre's mobile number. She answered quickly and he reported the second break in.

"This is getting to be a habit," she said. "I'll call the SOCO people and get some officers down there to interview the security staff again. I take it I don't have to remind you not to touch anything?" Hugh grimaced; of course they hadn't touched anything.

Matlock added, "Have you heard from the higher ups?"

"Not yet. But Francis is contacting them today about Robert's condition. He was found yesterday with his wife Virginia in a remote location. According to Francis he's in a bad condition mentally. Virginia and Ian have been feeding him drugs, but we don't know exactly what yet. Francis is waiting for the results of the tox screen before he knows for sure. Last we spoke to him, Robert was about to be assessed by a psychiatric doctor."

A sigh came over the phone. "You know Robert and I never completely saw eye to eye, but for something like this to happen to such an astute and intelligent man is heartbreaking."

Hugh could only agree. He and Robert were not exactly friends, but the other man had always had their backs when they were out in the field on jobs.

After ending the call, Hugh turned to Falcon. "Can you phone Francis and get an update on Robert? We'd best go downstairs and wait for the SOCOs to turn up. I'd like a word with the security guys anyway."

Falcon nodded and called his father. Hugh listened with half an ear to their conversation as he led the way back to the ground floor. He left Falcon talking to Francis and approached the security desk.

"Hi, Derek," he addressed the man behind the monitors. "Where's Jeff?"

Derek had straightened up when Hugh approached and was now looking at him in confusion.

"He just got a phone call from his wife and had to leave. Is there something wrong, Mr McHughes?"

Hugh sighed. Another coincidence? He thought not.

"The police will be here soon. There's been another break in at our offices." Derek gaped at him. "But–"

"Who was on duty last night?" Hugh interrupted.

"I was supposed to be me, but it was my wedding anniversary, and I wanted to take Linda out for a meal. Jeff stood in for me."

"Thanks, Derek. When you speak to Jeff will you let him know I need to have a word with him? The police will be here soon to take your statement and look at the crime scene."

"I will." Derek hesitated. "Sir, you don't think Jeff had anything to do with it, do you?"

"I'll leave that to the police to ascertain. I'm sure they'll arrange to interview him."

He left the security desk and made his way over to Falcon in the foyer. His phone still to his ear as he spoke to Francis. As Hugh approached him, he smiled as their eyes met. A frisson of excitement went through Hugh as he remembered the previous night. Falcon was one good looking man and, for the moment at least, he was all his. Hugh found himself hoping that they could have a long-term relationship. He found himself hoping that Falcon felt the same. He sat down next to his lover as the other man ended his call.

"Hey," Falcon greeted him, taking his right hand in his left and squeezing. "Dad says he visited Robert again this morning and he was a bit better, but still suffering from the aftereffects of the drugs. They're not sure how long it will be before they can get them out of his system. He's going through quite a nasty withdrawal at the moment."

Hugh nodded.

"The psychiatric assessment found that he wasn't really in control of his own thoughts and was showing signs of anxiety, depression and dissociating. They're keeping him under observation, especially whilst he's going through withdrawal."

Before he could say anything, Hugh's attention was drawn to the doors of the building. Several police officers had entered, along with the SOCOs. Thankful that DI Matlock had come with them, he and Falcon got up to greet them.

#

Falcon

They'd been in Manchester for a few days and the change in Imogen's condition was noticeable. Falcon followed Hugh into her hospital room on Sunday morning, and she was sitting up in bed enjoying a cup of tea. The fun-loving woman he'd first met in York weeks ago was beginning to make a reappearance.

"How are you this morning, gorgeous?" Hugh asked as he leant down to kiss her cheek. She beamed up at him as he stepped aside, so Falcon too could kiss her in greeting.

"Doing a lot better," she answered, settling back against her pillows. "The doctors have already done their rounds and have given me the green light to be discharged tomorrow."

"No wonder you're grinning," Hugh replied from his seat near the bed. "No Luci this morning?"

"No, I finally persuaded her to go to my apartment to get a proper night's sleep and a shower, and to relax. She'll be back by teatime."

"Good," Hugh replied. "She needed a break but funny enough, she's as stubborn as you are."

Imogen laughed, though she winced slightly, which still showed how hurt she was after the accident.

"Any news from the police?" she asked next.

"I spoke to Matlock last night. They found the driver of the lorry who crashed into you. He states he was hired anonymously through an app. He doesn't know anything about who hired him. The IT geeks are trying to hack the app but not having any luck so far. He's in prison, denied bail until he appears before the bench on Monday next week," reported Hugh.

She nodded as she returned her cup to the tray in front of her. Falcon could see the cost of the accident, not just the physical, but the mental as well.

"Have you decided on Paris?" he asked her to take her mind off things. "Yes. Luci insists. I'm not one to turn down a visit to Paris and my sister's apartment, so I'll go back with her when I'm discharged and stay for a few days at least."

"Good," Hugh replied. "The break will be good for you. Why don't you go visit Villefranche-sur-Mer whilst you're there? You know you enjoy the sea there. The villa is always available for you."

Imogen's eyes lit up at the mention of a villa. Falcon turned to face Hugh. "I didn't know you had a villa in the south of France."

"Hmm." Hugh turned to him and smiled. "I'll take you

later in the summer if you want? It was my mum's, she inherited it from her mother, who was French. Since Mum and Dad prefer Spain, she signed it over to me."

Falcon smiled. He was happy that Hugh was beginning to think of a future for them, but also that he was learning new things about his lover. He was a quarter French; somehow, he found that incredibly sexy.

"Do you speak the language?"

"*Mais oui*!" Hugh laughed. "We actually lived there for about five years when we were little, Dad was working for the French branch of his company. I went to a local school and played with the local kids. Even now when I go back, I always visit Armand and his family."

There was a knock on the door and the police officer on duty – a young man Falcon hadn't seen before – came in. Unusually, he shut the door behind him.

"Yes?" Hugh asked as he stood up.

The young man pulled a taser he'd been holding behind his leg. He was sweating and appeared to be having trouble holding taser steady.

"I'm s–s–sorry, sir," he gasped out, reaching behind him to open the door again.

In shock, Falcon watched as Ian Swales entered the room, a super pissed off look on his face.

"Now look at what you've made me do," he hissed as he entered the room.

Falcon ignored him, trying to get a look out into the corridor. He could just make out a couple of other men dotted around, and the nurses and other staff also held at gun or taser point.

"Ian!" Hugh said in disgust. "Do you really think you can get away with this?"

"If only you'd done your job properly in the first place, McHughes, then none of this would have been necessary!"

"Still blaming others for your shortcomings, I see," Hugh replied.

Falcon wanted to tell him to stop aggravating the man, but at the same time, the longer he kept Swales talking the more time it gave the police to arrive. He was sure the nursing staff would have already used the emergency button. He wondered what had happened to the policeman outside Gil's room.

He looked at the young policeman near the door, who was still sweating. His taser trembled in his hand as he tried to cover all three of them in the room. Ian glanced over at him, sighed and pointed his gun at the young officer. Suddenly, a muffled shot rang out and the officer dropped to the floor with a bullet in his neck.

Imogen screamed and Hugh jumped forward, putting himself in front of both Falcon and Imogen.

"What the fuck!" he shouted.

Ian calmly turned his gun back to them and gestured to Hugh to come closer. "I think it's time you came with me."

Falcon gaped at him. What was this?

"Why?" he blurted out before he could stop himself.

Ian scowled at him. "I need one of you to show me how to find the treasure. With you two contained, Hugh can show me where it is in York."

"You're mad," Imogen said, glaring at the man who was the very image of her boss.

"Be careful," Falcon whispered to her. "Now!" Ian shouted at Hugh.

Hugh reached behind him and squeezed the hand Falcon held out to him twice.

That was their prearranged signal, and Falcon got ready to protect Imogen as Hugh put his head down and ran full tilt into Ian's stomach. Before Ian could discharge his gun, Hugh had him down on the ground, banging his hand on the floor trying to dislodge the gun from his grip.

Outside the room, Falcon could hear a commotion. It sounded as though the police had arrived. Hopefully they were armed.

A florid man entered the room and pushed Hugh off Ian, pulling the older man back with him.

"Boss!" he said as he got Ian on his feet, his gun firmly pointed at Hugh. "The police are here. We have to go!"

Ian grunted then pointed his gun at Hugh and pulled the trigger.

Imogen screamed and Falcon launched himself at Hugh to push him out of the way. There was noise and scrambling, as Ian and the other man rushed from the room. Then there was a pocket of silence.

Falcon, his heart in his mouth, pushed himself off Hugh. He examined him all over, hearing Hugh's groan as he tried to sit up.

"I'm okay, Fal," he assured him. "He just winged me."

By this time, Imogen had got out of bed and was holding a wad of paper towels to Hugh's arm. DI Matlock appeared at the door and nodded when she saw what was happening. She shouted for help and one of Imogen's young doctors appeared. Hannah dropped down next to Hugh and Falcon and gently removed the paper towels from Hugh's arm.

"Okay, you'll have to come with me, Mr McHughes. It looks like the bullet went through the fleshy part of your arm, but I need to check to make sure."

Hugh tried to argue with her, but Falcon helped him to

stand, took him into his arms and trying not to hurt his arm, squeezed him tight. He was still trembling, and needed the assurance that Hugh was indeed okay.

"Go with the nice doctor," he instructed his lover, reluctantly letting him go. "I'll stay here."

Falcon stayed with Imogen as Hugh left the room with the doctor, then the police descended on them and removed the body of the poor young officer.

#

Four hours later, Imogen had been moved to a different room. Lucinda had arrived back and been horrified at what had happened. Hugh was back from seeing the doctor, and his left arm was bandaged where he'd had several stitches. Fortunately, the bullet had missed anything important. The corridor outside Imogen's old room had been designated a crime scene. Several SOCOs were still around taking fingerprints and photographing the room. Gil fortunately was unharmed in his own room, Swales's men hadn't entered the room, just disabled the policeman on duty.

"I think I've seen more of the British police in the last few days than in the rest of my life," Imogen remarked to Hugh. "I think that's more than enough for anyone! I've spoken to DI Matlock, and she's arranged for us to leave Manchester airport for Paris tonight, under police protection."

Falcon had been there for that conversation. Imogen and Lucinda had been grateful for the offer, though they'd tried to argue that they didn't need it.

Matlock had also arranged for a local police officer to meet them in Paris and for protection at Lucinda's apartment. They all hoped it wouldn't be needed.

"Do we know anything about the young officer who was killed yet?" Hugh asked.

"Yes, he wasn't supposed to be on duty today. The woman who was supposed to be on duty had been called home by her mother when someone broke into their house early this morning. He'd agreed to take her place. His name was Jon Buckley, and he was only 24. How he got mixed up with Ian and his lot we still don't know."

Hugh nodded. He still looked pale and Falcon decided it was time to head back to the apartment.

"Time to go," he said.

Lucinda nodded. "Yes, take him home, Fal. I'll phone you when we get to Paris. And you..." She turned to Hugh with tears in her eyes. "Take care and watch your step. Ian's getting desperate. I can't believe he managed to escape given how many police descended on the place."

Falcon agreed that there was something shady about that, but he knew that DI Matlock was investigating.

There was a flurry of goodbyes and promises to be careful on all sides.

Eventually, Falcon managed to get Hugh out of the hospital and hustled him to their car, nodding at the waiting policeman that would follow them out of the hospital car park.

They weren't taking any chances. For the moment, they were all under police protection.

Chapter Nineteen

Hugh

Hugh hissed as he moved his arm whilst getting in the shower. He'd wrapped cling film around it to protect the wound from the water. Fortunately, it was his left arm as he was right-handed. It still hurt when he moved it in the wrong way though.

"You okay?" Falcon asked as he joined Hugh, picking up the shower gel to help. "Just a bit sore."

"I'll change the bandage when we've finished here." Falcon smiled at him as he spread shower gel over his chest. Only yesterday morning a similar move had led to a make out session, but this morning they were a bit more restrained.

After quickly washing both their hair, Falcon rinsed them both off. Getting out, he handed Hugh a towel whilst he wandered into the bedroom to dry off and get ready for the day. Hugh watched him go, enjoying the view.

Once half dressed, Hugh moved to the kitchen where Falcon had a bandage and other supplies laid out on the counter. Hugh had kept his shirt off ready for his arm to be re-bandaged. Falcon was gentle as he peeled off the old bandage and examined his wound.

"The bruising is starting to come out now," he said.

Hugh twisted, trying to see the back of his arm where the bullet had exited. He couldn't quite see, but he trusted Falcon to tell him if there were any problems.

It hadn't been the first time he'd been shot, but it wasn't something you ever got used to. He flexed his arm a bit before Falcon wrapped it up once more. Only another day or so and he'd be able to leave the bandage off. The stitches should dissolve as well.

Pouring coffee from the carafe on the side, the couple set about preparing breakfast and getting the day on the go. They'd heard from Lucinda earlier this morning to say that she and Imogen were safely back at her apartment with a gendarme on duty outside the apartment block. They intended to stay only for a few days before heading off to Villefranche-sur-Mer for a couple of weeks. Hugh envied them that part of the proceedings; it had been a while since he'd last visited his villa there. He was looking forward to taking Falcon there once everything had been sorted out.

Gil was still in the hospital, after having been hit by a fever a couple of days after the accident. They'd had to put antibiotics in his IV line to help him. He was getting better, but they wanted to keep him in for a couple more days, to be sure.

Hugh looked up as Falcon's phone rang and smiled when he greeted the person on the other end.

"Percy! Say you have something for us." He tapped his phone screen. "Hang on, just putting you on speaker with Hugh."

"Hi Hugh," Percy called. "How are you today?"

Hugh replied, updating them on the last few days and confirming that his wound was getting better.

"I'm glad your friend made it to Paris okay," Percy said. "Are you heading back to York soon?"

"Today," Falcon confirmed.

"Oh good, any chance you can do a detour?"

"Where had you in mind?"

"Leconfield Hall?" Percy replied. "I'd suggest somewhere in between, but I'm really busy at the moment and can't leave for too long. It would be great if you could come here. We'll treat you to a cream tea!"

Hugh laughed. "How can we resist! I'm sure we can make a detour to Leconfield before returning to York. I'd love to see your home."

Percy laughed too. "Would you be able to get here for 1 pm?"

"I'm sure we can," Hugh replied, looking at the clock to see it was 9.30 am. "If we set off in the next hour, we should make it to you between 12.30 and 1 pm."

"Good. I'll let the others know. Andrew and Walker will be joining us. There's quite a bit to tell, but I don't want to get into it over the phone."

They wrapped up the call then began getting ready to go. Falcon's car, which Hugh had driven to Manchester, was still parked in the underground parking area of his apartment building. They agreed to take that one to York and leave Hugh's there for now.

An hour later, they were on the M62 heading towards Hull and then Leconfield. As Falcon drove, Hugh spoke to DI Matlock on the phone. She explained to him about the working group that had been set up between North Yorkshire Police and Manchester Police to work on their related cases.

"Jack Speight, your contact at York," Matlock was saying now, "has just been promoted to Detective Constable and will be the liaison between yourselves and the working group. I understand you know him from the army, Hugh?"

"I do, Jack's a good one. I'll contact him once we're back in York."

"You'll be there tonight?"

"Should be, otherwise tomorrow. I don't think we'll stay over in Leconfield but just in case."

"I'll keep you in the loop. Keep your phone on and report anything strange to myself and Speight."

Hugh could hear the worry in Matlock's voice, so he didn't react to her laying the law down as he would have normally done. Instead, he agreed to keep in touch and ended the call.

"Services coming up. Do you want to stop?" Falcon asked as they approached the Ferrybridge services on the M62.

"Quick pit stop for coffee," he replied, and Falcon flicked the indicator on to come off at the next exit. Hugh could do with the caffeine and maybe some carbohydrates as well.

#

Just over an hour later, they turned left into the long driveway towards Leconfield Hall. The entrance was just opposite what had been RAF Leconfield years ago and was now an army driver training base.

They drove down close to the house. Falcon bypassed the public car park and continued to a small visitor and staff car park.

Standing out on the driveway waiting for them was a teenage boy. Falcon pointed him out to Hugh, telling him he was Pollie's nephew, Bertie. The young lad grinned when he saw Falcon and waved at them.

"Uncle Fal!" he exclaimed as they got out of the car and walked towards him. "Percy said to take you to the café and he and Walker will be with you soon. I'm to buy you whatever you want for lunch."

Hugh grinned at the enthusiastic, lanky youth. Falcon introduced them and they followed their guide to the café where they were greeted by Phil the chef. Once they were settled, Bertie left them to their lunch, and they enjoyed the ambiance of sitting in the old conservatory. Falcon explained the changes that had been made in the last couple of years, including the conservatory entrance way becoming the café.

"Here they are," Hugh said as Percy and another man walked up. Falcon stood up to greet him.

"Walker, great to see you again." He shook the other man's hand then introduced the red-haired man to his lover.

"Hugh, this is Walker Brown. He's a medieval scholar, but also our go-to when we need any historical research carrying out."

"It's great to meet you, Walker." Hugh said standing up and shaking his hand, and then Percy's. "No Andrew?"

"He's waiting for us in the conference room. We thought we'd let you get lunch out of the way. If you've finished?"

"Yes, we're done," Hugh replied.

#

Falcon

Falcon followed Hugh into the conference room and grinned at Andrew who was sitting at the table waiting for them.

"Hey," he greeted, shaking his hand as he got up. "How are you doing?"

"I'm okay, thanks," Andrew replied, sitting back down after shaking Hugh's hand as well. "It was the shock of my two worlds colliding that affected me the other day. I've had some time to put everything into perspective since then.

"We were sorry to hear about your friend, Hugh. How's the arm?" he went on to ask.

"Not so bad," Hugh replied, grimacing slightly. Falcon watched him carefully, aware he didn't always admit to being in pain. "It catches every now and again, but it'll be okay. I've just taken some more painkillers."

Andrew nodded and took the bottle of water Walker held out to him. Hugh and Falcon shook their heads when he offered them bottles as well as they'd both just had a big pot of tea between them and didn't feel the need for more liquid.

As they all settled at the table, Falcon looked around the room. He'd never been in the conference room here before and was interested in some of the boards from old exhibitions that were propped against walls. He'd also noted several documents and a couple of old books on the table in front of Walker as well. He hoped they had good news for them.

"Any luck?" he asked, indicating the books and documents on the table.

Walker grinned at him. "Yes, for once we've managed to track down a couple of things that we think will be of interest to you and might even help you with your vampire problem."

Falcon laughed at that. It was great to see Walker so enthused; he did love his research. In recent years, he'd worked at York University in their history department. Before that, he'd been in demand as a visiting lecturer all over the world.

"It's good to have you on our side." Falcon grinned back at him.

Walker nodded and picked up a slim volume from the table. "We got lucky with this volume. It was in a collection we acquired a couple of years ago."

The small volume was obviously old, and Walker held it out for Falcon to take. He looked it over and opened it up. The frontispiece declared it to be *On the History of Vampires* and it was dated 1755. He flicked through the pages, but a lot of the writing was old and flowery, and he had difficulty making sense of it.

"Here." Andrew held his hand out and Falcon passed him the book. "This section is the bit we found interesting." He passed the book back.

Falcon took it and with Hugh looking over his shoulder, he read the chapter title:

On Sleeping Vampires. He drew in a breath and looked at Andrew. "Is this what I think it is?"

"Yep. We believe this is where Gilead got the spell from that put the vampire in the tunnel room to sleep. There's also one further on that talks about forcing an already sleeping vampire awake."

"It could be just what we need to help the vampire in the sarcophagus," Hugh spoke up, his eyes alight with the possibilities. "Have you read through it? Does it seem as though it would work?"

"We think it should." Walker sounded more cautious than Andrew had been. "But you'll need to enlist the help of another vampire. Since you have Francis around that should be no problem."

Falcon sighed with relief. Yes, Francis would help and he

and his brothers plus Hugh should have enough magical resonance between them to work the spell.

"Here." Walker handed him a print-out of the chapter in question, with the two spells outlined. Falcon thanked him.

"I'll also email it to you," he added.

"That's just brilliant, Walker, thank you so much. Do we know how Gilead got hold of the spell in the first place?"

"We do," Andrew answered. "When we got back from visiting with you in York, I was determined to find out what happened to Gilead after I met him. It's a bit of a sad story. I told you he was being blackmailed about his homosexuality by the *Hispana Nonus*," he recapped. "It turned out they weren't the only ones. A young man with a grudge against him turned him into the police in Hull after a night spent together in one of the inns there. He was sentenced to 14 months in prison.

"He died not long after his sentence and left his considerable collection of antiquities and documents in the trust of his long-term housekeeper. Unfortunately, she didn't long outlive him, and it reverted to his nephew, who put it all up for sale. It was sold off in lots and went to various corporations and private collectors."

"How sad," Hugh muttered.

"It was," Andrew agreed. "The bright side is that a lot of his collection is in the local History Centre in Hull and the East Riding archives in Beverley, for people to be able to see. This volume though..." He held up the small book again. "This came to us by a different route. Gilead was a member of the *Hull Literary and Philosophical Society* and also a member of the subscription library that was based in Albion Street in Hull. It had a large collection of books, including a good collection of magic theory history and practical volumes. We believe Gilead found it there and copied out the relevant information on the spell. After the library got into financial difficulties at the beginning of the 20th century, many of their books, including this one, were sold off."

"Wasn't that the place that was destroyed during the 2nd World War?" Hugh asked, sitting forward.

"It was," Percy agreed. "In 1943. Lots of artefacts were buried, though some were recovered on a dig in 1989, called appropriately enough *The Phoenix Project.* They were able to recover several artefacts and return them to the museum's authority."

Falcon could tell that Hugh was fascinated by this history and he promised himself that they'd follow up on it a bit more when they had more time. For now, he needed to get the spells to Francis to see what he thought.

"I've forwarded your email to Francis," he told Walker. "We'll know what he thinks when we get back."

"I guess that means we should start making our way to York," Hugh grumbled.

Falcon laughed. "I promise you that when we're not involved in a situation like this, you can come back and discuss history and research with Walker all you like."

Hugh grinned at him, leaning in for a kiss. "Thank you," he whispered against his lips.

Falcon returned the kiss, then checking his phone, stated that they really must be going. Francis had sent him a quick text to thank him for the email and inviting them to a family dinner the following night to discuss next steps. He showed Hugh who grunted in reply. Falcon smiled internally, he knew his brothers would love Hugh, and he'd already met two of them.

They stood up and Percy was called away by his assistant

Manon to help her with a query, so Walker and Andrew walked them out.

"Don't be strangers." Walker grinned, shaking Hugh's then Falcon's hands again. "I'm sorry you didn't get to see Pollie and the baby, but she's over visiting Cris's parents with Nathan. They love her and baby Emma but have difficulty getting their heads around our relationship, so only Cris and Nathan go with them now."

Falcon nodded. He could see where some people might have problems with a harem relationship, but to him if everyone was happy, that was good enough.

"Maybe next time," he replied as he and Hugh got into his car. He turned round and waved at them as they made their way down the long driveway to the main road, before heading to join the A1079 to York.

"You okay?" he asked Hugh who had gone quiet.

"Hmm, what? Sorry," Hugh replied absently. "Just thinking about meeting all your family in one go tomorrow night."

"You're not nervous, are you?"

"Just a bit."

"Don't be." Falcon rested his hand on Hugh's knee. "I'm sure they'll all love you."

"Yeah, yeah," Hugh replied. He reached over and switched some music on.

Falcon knew that though Hugh's parents were still alive, he was an only child and didn't have any siblings, or from what he could gather, any cousins either. He determined that Hugh could share his siblings, he certainly had enough to go around.

Chapter Twenty

Hugh

Hugh relaxed back into the driver's seat, following Falcon's directions to Francis's house in Knapton, a small village just off the York ring road. They were heading over there for the family meal and meeting that Francis had called. Saturday afternoon in the last week of May was proving to be quite hot as they negotiated the ring road and pulled off on to the main road through Knapton.

"You have to go through the village and almost out the other side," Falcon said, smiling as the air through the open windows blew his hair about. "It's the last house on the right."

Hugh followed the directions and indicated to pull into a fairly large driveway with enough room for several cars. Which was good, given how many were already parked there.

"Good," Falcon said. "Jenny is here with her brood. I've not seen Foster for some time now."

"That's her husband, right?"

"Yep. They've been married almost 20 years. You've met two of the triplets, Ella and Abbie. You'll get to meet Cory, their brother, today."

They got out of the car, just as another pulled into the driveway. Hugh saw that Raven was driving and Robin was in the passenger seat. At least he knew these two brothers. He and Falcon stepped to one side.

"Bro." Robin greeted Hugh with a hug, then with a grin, held out a hand to Hugh, who shook it. Raven did the same.

"Looks like everyone else is here," Falcon said as Hugh felt his warm hand rest on his back and direct him towards the rear of the house. "They'll be round the back on the patio."

Hugh nodded and allowed Falcon to steer him, with the brothers following on behind. When they rounded the house, they were greeted with a flurry of kisses and handshakes, and Hugh was introduced to the rest of the brothers. Piper, or Pip as he preferred to be called, was a short muscular man. His skin had overtones of mahogany, and he pulled Falcon into a hug. Nix, short for Phoenix, towered over both Hugh and Falcon, his long, wavy, brown hair cascading around his shoulders. Oleander, or Ollie, was next to greet them. He was as short as Pip, but wiry with it. His hair was red, and his green eyes seemed to bore into Hugh's soul.

"Okay, okay, everyone, that's enough. Let the guy have a seat and a drink," Francis yelled over the hubbub. Everyone laughed and Hugh found himself being led to a comfortable seating area next to Abbie and her siblings.

"Hugh!" Abbie all but squealed as she got up to greet him with a quick embrace and a kiss on his cheek. She turned to who Hugh assumed were her parents and introduced him.

"I'm so pleased to meet you," Jenny said, holding her hand out. Hugh shook hers, then her husband's and greeted Ella.

He was then introduced to Cory who told him he worked with Nix at his antiques shop.

"Here." Falcon joined him on the sectional and handed him a cold beer. He quickly gulped down about half of it before putting it on the table in front of him. No, of course he hadn't been nervous about meeting the rest of the family.

"Dinner's ready, come and get it!" Francis called. There was a wave of movement towards Francis and Ollie at the bar-be-que. The food was laid out on the table next to them: salads, bread, burgers, chicken legs and sausages. They all loaded up and returned to the seating area.

Conversation was casual as they ate. Several of the brothers asked Hugh how Imogen was doing, and he was able to report that he'd spoken to her that morning and that she was fine. She and Lucinda would be making their way to Villefranche-sur-Mer the next day to spend several days in Hugh's villa there.

After dessert, Jenny, London and the triplets said they had to be making their way back. Everyone waved them off from the driveway and Hugh realised their car had been parked so they could get out first.

"A long time ago, Jenny decided she didn't want to get involved in the paranormal investigative side of things. It's why we don't discuss it at meals and wait until she and her family has left before we begin talking about it," explained Falcon.

Hugh nodded. He could understand that. He leant back against his lover, letting him take his weight as he watched the small family leave, waving with the others. They then all made their way back to the patio and helped to clear up.

Afterwards, coffees in hands, they all settled in the great room in Francis's house. It was large and airy, with French doors opening out on to the garden. Francis had placed the print-outs from the pictures Falcon had forwarded to him from Walker in front of him.

"Have you had time to study them?" Falcon asked his father. Francis nodded as he passed a copy around for everyone to see.

"I have. I must admit I am once again impressed by Walker's research ability. Did you say he found this in a new collection?"

"He didn't go into too much detail, but I got the impression it had been in the hands of the Witch Megginson before her death."

Francis nodded and Hugh raised an eyebrow at Falcon in question. He whispered he would explain more later.

"It's kind of worrying that something like this exists," Nix spoke up for the first time.

Francis nodded. "You're right, son. Still, at least the person who wrote this spell also gave the counter spell."

"He did?" Hugh sat up. "That's great news. Does that mean we can help the vampire stuck in the sarcophagus?"

"Certainly," Francis replied. "Though it will take careful manouevering. When this vampire wakes up, he'll be hungry, and his thirst will be high. We'll have to make sure there's a good source of blood for them to ingest. Otherwise, it could become very nasty if they attacked whoever was there in a blood lust."

The others agreed, and Hugh was particularly worried, he appeared to be the only one nervous about waking the sleeping vampire. They spent the next hour or so discussing what they could do to mitigate any attack on them when they woke them.

"Is there a chance you might know who it is, Dad?" Ollie

asked his father.

"A good chance. It's why I've waited for Falcon and Hugh to get back to York, so they can take me into the room again and I can see if I recognise them."

"We've been keeping an eye on the various entrances to the tunnels," Robin spoke up then. "We scared someone away from one entrance the other night. Not sure if he was connected to Ian Swales but we weren't taking any chances."

"Whose watching them now?" Hugh asked.

"Some friends of ours. We didn't explain about them, just that they needed to watch the areas and call one of us if anyone got too close to them."

Hugh nodded. "I wish we had a better map of the whole area. I know there's the one Father John left us, but it's incomplete."

"It is," Francis agreed. "Robin, did you get hold of what I requested?"

The younger man grinned and said he'd be right back. Francis refused to answer any questions until he returned, and instead offered everyone a refill on their coffee.

Robin came back in carrying a strange-looking wheel contraption. He was still grinning, now from ear to ear, as he put it on the floor and wheeled it towards them.

"It measures distance," he announced, showing them the black box on the side where they could see the readout panel.

"It's an odometer," Pip spoke up. "I remember seeing the surveyor using one at the Walk. He was measuring out where everything was going to fit when he took over the shops."

"Got it in one!" Robin exclaimed, wheeling it around the room and putting it through its paces. "Isn't it wonderful!"

Hugh grinned too, catching some of the younger man's

enthusiasm. He could see him as the mischievous little boy that Falcon had described to him.

"It is great," he said. "You're right there. So, do I take it we're going to use it to measure and map the tunnels?"

"Exactly," Francis replied to Hugh. "I thought you, Falcon and Robin could do that while the rest of us put a plan into action to rescue the sleeping vampire."

They continued to discuss things for another hour or so, but nothing new was being said, so they all agreed to call it a night. Yawning, Hugh looked at his phone to see that it was nearly midnight. Where had the time gone!

Making a plan to meet up with Robin the next day, they took their leave. Falcon grabbed the keys from Hugh and said he'd drive. Hugh grinned. He hadn't drunk that much, but if Fal felt better driving, then he'd let him.

#

Falcon

Falcon soared above the moors entwined with Raven, in his mind, as his brother flew high. They were taking the opportunity of a bit of freedom from the facility and enjoying the flight. Falcon ignored his body which was strapped to a medical chair in the laboratory.

For the moment they were free.

"Over there!" Falcon whispered to Raven, who changed direction and swooped over towards the coast.

They played on the wind for a while, their troubles forgotten for the moment. Suddenly Falcon felt Raven falling out of the air. His brother cawed in surprise, then screamed in agony. Falcon was ripped from him.

Sucking in a deep breath, he screamed. He was back in the facility, strapped to the bed, and was freaking out.

"Raven! Raven!" he cried out, thrashing against his restraints, trying to get free. "Stop it, boy!" The disembodied voice came over the speaker.

"Nooooooo!" he screamed. "Falling. Falling!"

"Somebody shut him up!" The voice was full of impatience.

Falcon struggled harder as one of the orderlies came into the room. He pinched Falcon's cheeks hard.

"Behave," he growled.

Falcon shook his head again, writhing backwards and forwards, fighting against his restraints. The orderly slapped him and told him again to be quiet. But he couldn't. He was lost in the feeling of Raven falling out of the sky. He couldn't reach him, couldn't connect.

"Here." The orderly shoved a gag into Falcon's mouth. "That'll shut you up."

Falcon tried to pull in another deep breath through his mouth, but he couldn't get any air into his lungs. He began choking and gasping for air…

#

"Falcon! Falcon!" Hugh's concerned voice pulled Falcon from his nightmare. He sat up quickly, pulling much needed air into his lungs. He was still screaming.

"It's okay, I've got you," Hugh whispered in his ear. He'd pushed up onto his knees and was holding Falcon in his arms.

Tears streaming down his face, Falcon allowed Hugh to comfort him. One of his brothers or Francis had always been there to comfort him after they'd been rescued from the facility, but it felt nice to be ensconced in Hugh's arms now.

"Ssshhh, I've got you. It'll be okay."

He listened to Hugh's comforting words for a while, before

taking another shuddering breath and laying back down. Hugh continued to hold him.

"Do you want to talk about it?"

Falcon took in another gulping breath before turning onto his side. Hugh moved to lie opposite him, his hand splayed out on his thigh. Falcon looked deep into the other man's eyes and knew he'd really lucked out here.

"I…" He hesitated. "It was during the years we spent at the facility. They were experimenting with various things to enhance the connection between myself and Raven. He was flying over the moors when he suddenly fell out of the air. I was along for the ride and felt him in pain, then falling…"

Hugh stroked his hair, giving him comfort and time to gather his thoughts. "When I came back to myself at the facility I was screaming and trying to breathe. To stop me from making too much noise, one of the orderlies eventually put a gag on me and I started choking. No-one would let me know about Raven."

He shuffled closer to Hugh, hiding his face in his neck. Even now he could feel the fear that something bad had happened to his brother.

"He was okay?" Hugh asked.

Falcon nodded. "Yes, he'd fallen out of the sky, but had managed somehow to control it. One of his wings was broken. They went out in the van and collected him. When he shifted back to human, his right arm was broken." He gulped. "It was a bad break. He couldn't shift for months."

"How old were you?"

"I was 16, Raven was 13. Fortunately, a few months later, Francis arrived to rescue us and take us home with him."

They lay there for a while taking comfort from each other. Shortly afterwards, he felt himself drifting off again.

***

#

The next morning, Falcon was suffering from a headache, so he quite readily agreed to let Hugh go and meet Robin on his own. He would join them later when his head was clearer. He slept for another few hours and woke up feeling a lot better. Stumbling into the kitchen, he found that Falcon had left coffee for him and some bagels were waiting by the toaster for his breakfast. He smiled at his boyfriend's thoughtfulness before he pulled Raven's number up on his phone and pressed call.

"Hey, bro!" Raven's voice came over the speaker. "How are you feeling this morning."

"You've seen Hugh?"

Raven laughed. "No, spoke to Robin a couple of hours ago. He said you were having a lie in as you had a bad headache."

"Oh."

"Really…" Raven's voice lowered in concern. "Are you okay?"

"I am now," Falcon replied, taking his coffee and bagel to the kitchen nook. "I had the dream again last night. The one where you were falling."

"Damn! It's been a while."

"I know. I think it's because there's been such a lot going on. The stress must have got to me."

There was a knock on his door then and to Falcon's surprise, Raven walked in. Falcon ended the call on his phone.

"Hey, bro," he greeted him, opening his arms wide for a hug. "I'm okay," Raven assured him. "You know I am."

"I know. But even after twenty years, it still scares me."

Raven didn't say anything, just gave him an extra hard hug before pulling away to go and pour himself some coffee.

"He's good for you, then?" "Hugh?" asked Falcon.

"Yes. Seems a good type of bloke."

"He is. He was really there for me last night. I think he might be the one, Venn."

Raven grinned back at him. "I hope so. You've had a long dry spell."

Falcon laughed. "You could say that. Trina was my last long-term relationship and that was five years ago. And we know what happened then."

"Did I tell you I saw her a couple of months ago?" Raven joined his brother in the kitchen nook.

"No. Do tell."

"She was in Coney Street and stopped to say hello. She asked after you. I got the feeling she regretted what had happened."

"Too late for that," Falcon muttered, remembering the bubbly woman who had captivated him for months. Before cheating on him with the brother of a mutual friend.

"Are she and Adam still together?"

"I don't know. I didn't ask."

Falcon dismissed thoughts of his ex. He wasn't interested anymore. Hugh held all his attention now. He just fitted with him, with him *and* his family.

"I'd best be getting back." Raven finished his coffee and stood up. "We're expecting a delivery, and I've left Aidan in charge."

Falcon liked Raven's assistant Aidan. The older man had been somewhat of a mentor for Raven when he was learning the business.

Falcon embraced his brother one more time and saw him

out of the flat, before turning and heading to the bathroom for his shower. Time to get the day under way.

Chapter Twenty-One

Hugh

Hugh and Robin were having fun mapping the tunnels with the odometer. They'd started at the Minster after Francis got the entrance opened temporarily so they could access that tunnel directly. Once they'd finished the mapping, the Minster would be closing that entrance completely. The Chapter had been very surprised to hear about the tunnels, even though Francis hadn't given them the complete story. He had told them that Father John had known about them since he was a young man. One of the older Canons had been set the task of trying to find any records or notes relating to previous knowledge of the tunnels and rooms under the Minster.

John's funeral had come and gone whilst Hugh and Falcon had been in Manchester with Imogen. Robin had represented his brothers and attended with his father. The two of them had kept an eye out for Swales, or any of his associates, but none of them had turned up, for which Francis was grateful.

Robin was measuring and Hugh was noting down the

direction of the tunnels from the one at the Minster. So far, they'd found a couple of small offshoots that ended in dead ends where the bedrock and been scraped but not dug out completely. All the time Hugh was keeping his eyes peeled for spell traps. He hadn't found any yet, but didn't want either himself or Robin to fall into one.

They had just left the Minster and were going to head toward the entrance in the boiler room on Ogilvy Street when Robin looked at his phone and grinned.

"Text from Falcon. He's up. Shall I ask if he wants to meet us?"

"Good idea. Tell him to meet us at the ice cream stand near the Minster," Hugh said, gesturing to the stand in front of them. "Come on, I'll treat you."

Robin grinned again and sent his brother the text. Hugh bought three ice creams, and they sat on one of the benches along the walkway behind the Minster. It wasn't long before Falcon joined them. Hugh handed over his ice cream.

"Thanks." He took the cone from him and settled back on the bench. They sat for a while enjoying their cold treats. Hugh looked around, remembering following Falcon through here a few weeks ago when he was going to meet Father McKenzie. He couldn't believe how much had happened since then. There was another school group visiting, and they moved around the grassy area before settling down to have their packed lunches. He remembered doing something similar himself as a schoolboy.

Robin, in the meantime, was showing Falcon the progress they'd made that morning and explaining the dead end tunnels to him.

"It's though they were being deliberate in leaving some of them like that," said Hugh, joining in the conversation.

"From the looks of it most of them are about the same age, but some of them are much, much older."

"Is it possible to tell how old?" Falcon asked.

"I'm not sure," Hugh answered. "It's not something I can tell. I think you'd maybe need an archaeologist to do some exploratory digging. Not sure how practical that would be."

They were quiet whilst they finished their ice creams, enjoying the mid-May sunshine. Then Robin picked up the odometer wheel and suggested they got on with the measuring.

They entered the tunnel through the old boiler room and immediately began to map out and measure the tunnel. As they got to where the rooms were, Hugh pulled out a builder's tape measure to help with getting the dimensions of the inner rooms.

"Is Francis joining us at any point?" Hugh asked.

"Dad said this morning he'd join us down here after lunch." Robin looked at his watch. "Shouldn't be too long now. I know he wanted to get a look at our vampire. He's hoping he knows them. It will help when we bring them out of their sleep, if we can put a name to them."

"Do you think it's okay to move them?" Hugh asked, drawing out where the doors in the sarcophagus room were.

"Dad seems to think it will be okay," Robin replied. "We had a good talk about it last night after you guys had left. I stayed over. It was just like old times."

Hugh laughed. "You mean you enjoyed being spoilt."

"I certainly did!" Robin agreed.

Falcon stopped what he was doing and listened. Hugh could hear something in the tunnels too.

He gestured for everyone to be quiet. It was most likely to be Francis, but he wasn't taking any chances. Even with Ollie and Raven monitoring the entrances that they knew about, they couldn't be too careful. He moved behind the open door, breathing slowly and quietly. The door creaked open a little more and Francis popped his head around it.

"Everything okay?" he asked.

There was an almost audible sigh around the room.

"Just being extra cautious," Falcon said, as he greeted his father.

"I don't blame you." Francis looked around the sarcophagus room with interest.

It was the first time he'd been in that room.

Hugh led the way over to the black sarcophagus and put his hand on the symbol on the front of the marble. The Latin inscription glowed as Hugh pressed down. The lid of the sarcophagus became opaque, allowing them to see the vampire in more detail.

Francis drew in his breath and whispered, "Malik!"

"You know him?" Falcon asked.

Francis nodded. "I had my suspicions as he disappeared around the time we're talking about. When I returned from Paris in the 1890s, I asked after him. None of the other vampires I knew had seen him for years. There was a suggestion he'd been killed, though I was hoping otherwise. He was turned about the same time I was. We were from different Greek states, and we fought against each other at the beginning. Then we fought together in many wars. We were in the same clan for a time, when vampires first gathered in clans for safety. Then he went one way and I another. We still tried to keep in touch, though. As much as you could in the days before there was a proper postal service."

Hugh whistled. "I can't get over how old you are."

Francis shrugged. "It's just getting on with your life, living each day as it comes. Same as anyone, really."

He continued, "I can't even begin to imagine what he's been going through."

"It's okay, Dad. We'll make sure he's alright before we wake him up."

Francis nodded, looking around the rest of the room in fascination. "Do we have any idea of what the *Hispana Nonus* were trying to do here?"

Hugh and the others shook their heads. "Not a clue."

#

Falcon

Falcon left Hugh and Robin to get on with measuring and mapping the tunnels. They'd brought Robin's laptop with his CAD program on it and were currently set up in the 'gentleman's club' room copying their morning's work on to it. He joined his father who was studying the sarcophagus.

"It's a remarkable piece of work," Francis said as he surveyed the hand carved marble. "It looks like part of it was originally used as a marble headstone. Amazing."

Falcon nodded and opened his inner eye to follow along with his father as he ran his hand over the marble. Several inscriptions were visible, many of them in Latin. He took out his phone and began writing the inscriptions down in a notes app, to investigate later. Maybe he'd send them to Percy and Walker, see what they made out of them.

"Do you think we will be able to safely extract him?"

"I think so. Though it will take careful manouevering to get the sarcophagus out of here and through the tunnels. It'll probably have to be done under cover of darkness. I wouldn't want to take him out of the sarcophagus until I've got something set up at the safe house near the Minster."

Falcon looked at the black marble and wondered how much it weighed. He groaned. They'd need a large dolly to move it down the corridors and it would take some going to get it up the stairs and through the boiler room.

"Sooner the better then," he said and made a note on his phone to hire a large dolly and find a way to weigh the marble.

"I agree." Francis continued to run his hand over the sarcophagus. "Robin?" he raised his voice a little.

"Yes?" Robin poked his head around the door.

"Let me have that tape measure you've got for a moment please. I need to measure this."

Robin handed the tape measure over and Falcon and Francis measured the sarcophagus. It was just under 2 metres in length, 1.2 metres in width and half a metre tall. Falcon wrote the details down, then returned the tape measure to his brother in the 'gentleman's club' room.

Francis joined them and sat in the wingback chair. Falcon could see that his father was sorting things out in his mind, likely making a plan to safely move the sarcophagus.

He wandered over to one of the bookshelves. *No time like the present,* he told himself. Whilst the others were engaged about their various tasks, he began pulling books off the shelves and looking at them. They all needed cataloging.

"What are you doing?" Hugh appeared at his shoulder a moment later, holding out a cold bottle of water to him.

"Thought I'd get a start on the cataloging," he answered, absently taking the water from his lover.

"Good idea." Francis stood up. "Maybe you'll find

something there that will help us work out why Malik is here, and how they put him into such a deep sleep."

"And why," Hugh put in.

Falcon nodded. He was very curious about that as well. What had happened that made the *Hispana Nonus* go to the trouble of getting a vampire, using a spell to put him to sleep, then just leaving him there for nearly two centuries? None of it made sense.

"What's the connection?" Hugh muttered and Falcon looked at him. "Connection?"

"Between these rooms, the *Hispana Nonus* and Ian Swales. Why is he interested?

What is it that draws him here?"

"It has to be something he can use," Francis mused, joining them. He chewed on a power bar and swallowed before he said anymore. "Ian was never one to be interested in the arcane and the paranormal. He was always the practical twin. So what was it that drew him here and why?"

"It doesn't make sense on the surface," Falcon agreed. "Something must have changed for him to be chasing this so hard."

"The only thing I can think of is that he came across something that mentioned the tunnels and probably something about what was down here. For all we know he has no interest in Malik at all and just wants the books or other artefacts that are down here."

"Hmm… I for one would love to corner him and find out. I can't fathom it otherwise," said Hugh.

"It's on my list of questions too," Francis replied, squeezing Hugh's arm, then hugging Falcon and Robin. "Well, I'm off to see if I can sort out some of the practicalities of moving Malik. Shall we meet up in your study later, Fal?"

They agreed to meet that evening about 7pm to share what they had discovered that day. Robin and Hugh went back to the CAD program and Falcon continued taking photos of the books, covers and inside front matter.

#

Falcon ordered pizza for their discussion that night and Ollie joined them, having handed over guarding the tunnels to Raven and Gray, a friend of theirs. They'd let them know if there was any action around any of the entrances. At least one thing had been confirmed that day – all the entrances were now mapped out and there weren't any they were unaware of.

Conversation was general as they ate the pizza, and the brothers enjoyed ribbing Falcon and Hugh about their burgeoning relationship.

"So, Hugh," Robin began, grinning, "when are you moving to York? As I can't see this one moving to Manchester!"

"Ha ha!" Falcon replied, grimacing. "We haven't talked about it yet, so keep your nose out, Rob!"

Secretly Falcon was hoping that Hugh would move to York. He was getting used to having the other man in his bed. Used to him being there in the morning, sharing breakfast with him and discussing the books they'd both read.

Hugh had gone red, and he coughed in embarrassment. "What he said! Though before I do anything else, I have to sort out whether I still have a job."

"Why's that?" Ollie asked.

"The agency no longer exists," Hugh replied. "The powers that be sent a text out to the whole team to tell us they were terminating the contract. Normally it would be up to Robert to decide what happens next, but it looks like he's not going to be in any kind of fit state to do that for some time to come."

Falcon leant in and kissed his boyfriend, not caring that his brothers were hooting and cat calling. Hugh needed the comfort only a lover could give. Falcon knew his job status had been bothering him, and he was also worried about Imogen and Gil's long-term futures. He put his hand on Hugh's cheek and looked into his eyes.

"We'll sort it," he assured him.

Hugh moved and kissed the palm of his hand. "Thank you."

"If it comes to it," Francis said, from where he was sitting opposite the couple, "I'd be happy to take both you and Gil on as paranormal investigators. Imogen too, if she'd be interested."

Hugh drew in a breath and turned to Francis. "Thank you for the offer. I'll think on it and mention it to the others. I'll get back to you."

"It's an open-ended offer, any time," Francis said kindly

Falcon wiped a stray tear from under Hugh's left eye. He knew the other man was completely touched by his father's offer. Hugh hadn't said too much about the situation, but he knew he'd been more worried about Gil and Imogen than he'd let on.

"Okay," Francis announced, putting his plate aside. "Time to get down to the business of moving Malik. I say the earlier the better, and to that end, I'd like to move tomorrow night."

Falcon drew in his breath. That was soon. "Can we be ready?" Robin asked.

"I wouldn't suggest it unless I thought it was doable," Francis answered his son. "Falcon has hired a large dolly to use to transport the sarcophagus. Raven has agreed to keep an eye on us from the sky, with Falcon along if needed."

"Where are we moving him to?" Hugh asked.

"We have a safe house not far from the Minster." It was Ollie who answered. "I've been checking out the best route from Ogleforth to there. We should be able to avoid most of the CCTV cameras and if we move at about 3 am, the streets should be practically deserted.

"I can help with that as well," Francis informed them. "If anyone sees us, I can use my vampire charm to convince them they didn't see a thing."

"Very useful." Hugh smiled.

"It is. I don't use it too often, but it can be a very handy skill."

They set to organising and working out the practicalities of moving Malik. Then, as they were tidying everything up and throwing rubbish out, there came a loud banging at the shop door.

Falcon immediately stood up and headed that way, closely followed by Hugh. As they got through the shop, they could see Jack Speight, the newly promoted Detective Constable at the door.

"Jack!" Hugh exclaimed as Falcon opened the door to let the other man it. "What is it?"

"Hugh. Been trying to reach you all night. Your phone not working?"

"We've had our phones on silent," Hugh said, as Jack followed them back to Falcon's study.

"What's going on, Jack?" Hugh asked, turning towards him.

The younger man took a deep breath. "I'm sorry but Gil Summers has been kidnapped by Swales's men."

"What! He was supposed to be under police protection!"

Hugh swore under his breath.

"He was," Jack replied sadly. "Both officers were knocked out and have severe concussions. They were lucky they didn't die."

Chapter Twenty-Two

Hugh

Hugh was still in shock at Jack's news when he walked into the conference room at the police station on Fulford Road. He'd had a sleepless night as he and Falcon had gone over and over the information that Jack had passed on about Gil's kidnapping.

#

"Whoever they are, they timed it just as Mr Summers was leaving the hospital. He's still on crutches. Here watch this."

Jack handed Hugh a tablet which was playing what had to be the hospital's own CCTV view of the exit. Gil came out on his crutches along with a couple of police officers. One was carrying Gil's bag. Hugh watched as a large Land Rover screamed to a stop in front of them and three hefty looking men got out. Their faces were covered and they carried cudgels. The police officer nearest to Gil went down first and Hugh winced as he watched the young woman's head bounce against the pavement.

The other officer was trying to protect Gil and use his radio at the same time. He had his truncheon out and was doing his best, but he was outnumbered by three to one. Once he was down, the three men picked up a struggling Gil and shoved him in the back of the Land Rover.

"That's awful," Hugh told Jack. He felt Falcon's hand in his and squeezed in response to the comfort offered. "Do you have any other information?"

"Not yet. Our officers have followed the Land Rover through some of the CCTV footage, but it was abandoned at the Arndale Centre, and it looks like they swapped cars there. No footage from the car park as the camera had been damaged earlier that day."

"Shit!" Hugh pulled his hands through his hair. Turning away, he began to pace. "What's your next step?" Falcon asked Speight.

"There's a full meeting tomorrow morning of the working group at Fulford Station. DI Matlock is coming over from Manchester. She suggested you both be there."

#

Hugh and Falcon were introduced to the rest of the team. When Matlock walked in, Hugh joined her at the table.

"Deidre," he greeted her by name. "Please tell me you have something."

She shook her head, looking pained. "I'm sorry Hugh," she replied. "There's nothing new to add."

He nodded and sat down in between Falcon and Jack Speight. Francis had offered to come with them, but they'd agreed he was better off organising Malik's move.

They'd had a bit of an argument over whether or not they should tell the police about the tunnels and the rooms they led to. It had been their first real disagreement, with Hugh stating it was difficult for the police to get a full picture of what was going on if they didn't know about the tunnels.

Falcon and Francis had successfully argued that moving Malik was a priority. Once that was done, they could let the police know about the tunnels, and how they'd found them, with the connection going back to Father McKenzie's death.

Hugh hadn't been completely happy with that. He had a good working relationship with DI Matlock and Jack was an old friend. He felt bad about keeping information from the police like this but agreed that Malik's safety should come first in this case.

One of the young PCs in the room was handing around coffee, tea or water to the attendees and Hugh grabbed a coffee. He needed the caffeine more than ever this morning.

"Have you heard from your counterpart in France?" Falcon asked Matlock. Hugh was grateful to him for thinking of Imogen and Lucinda.

"Lucinda and Imogen are both safe," she answered. "One of the first things we did was check in with the gendarme allocated to them in Villefranche-sur-Mer. They've doubled their presence but at the moment we don't believe Swales knows where they are."

"That's good." Hugh swallowed another mouthful of coffee. "Any update on your officers?"

DI Matlock smiled at him. "They're both doing fine, thanks for asking. They were kept in for observation overnight, but both have been released by the hospital now."

There were a couple of questions from some of the other officers in the working party about the places they knew where Ian Swales had been seen. They'd checked out all the places Robert owned, as well as the house the brothers had grown up in, which was still in the family's hands even though it had been empty for years. They'd spoken again to Robert's wife to try and see if she had any information as to where Ian had gone to ground, but there was nothing new.

A couple of hours later and they still hadn't made much progress. Hugh tried to stifle a yawn but couldn't succeed. He was worried for his friend, but last night's sleepless night was catching up with him. They'd have to get some sleep soon, or else they'd be useless helping with Malik's move.

DI Matlock wound the meeting up and came over to talk to Hugh and Falcon. "I'm really sorry this has happened Hugh. I like Gil and have always worked well with you and your agency. However, I get the feeling you're hiding something from me."

Hugh grimaced. "Nothing that will help find Ian," he replied carefully.

"Hmm. I'm off back to Manchester. If you think of anything that you'd like to share, you have my number."

She said goodbye to some of the other officers before leaving the room. Hugh turned to Falcon and suggested they go get some more sleep.

"Jack." He stopped his friend as he was leaving the room. "You'll keep us up to date?"

"I will, Hugh. Just make sure you keep your phone on this time!"

"I will, I promise," Hugh replied. He could see that Jack was as tired, if not more than they were. He'd been up half the night checking CCTV images.

"We'll be off then," Falcon said and steered Hugh out of the conference room. Outside the police station there was a chill in the air, and it looked like it was going to rain.

"Come on, let's go home and get some rest," said Falcon.

"Have you heard from your dad this morning?" asked Hugh.

"Yes, everything is going smoothly. We should have Malik in the safe house by this time tomorrow. Then we'll see if that spell Walker found will work."

Hugh nodded and followed Falcon to the car. They made their way back towards the city centre and St Mary's car park. From there it was only a short walk back to the bookshop.

When they got there, Abbie was sitting on her stool at the till, reading a book. But it was the customer who was coming from the back of the shop that held Hugh's attention. Abbie put her book down to greet the customer, but he rushed straight at Hugh and Falcon, knocking them to the ground.

"Hey!" Hugh cried out as he tried to stop the man. He recognised him as being at the hospital with Swales the day he'd turned up in Imogen's room. He scrambled to his feet.

"Abbie, call the police!" Falcon shouted at her and followed Hugh out of the shop.

The man hadn't got far, having run into Ollie outside his shop which was opposite Falcon's. Ollie had him down on the floor, his elbow in the man's back so he couldn't get up.

Fortunately, the police weren't long in coming. There was still protection around them, just not always visible. Obviously, that had been taken advantage of today.

"Got him," the young, plainclothes officer said as he cuffed the man, pulling him roughly to his feet. He handed him off to a uniformed officer to put in his nearby patrol car, parked on the pedestrianized Stonegate.

"I'll question him myself," the plainclothes officer said. He introduced himself, "Detective Constable Bill Turner."

He held out his hand and Falcon, Hugh and then Ollie shook it. "Is the young lady okay?" Turner asked, looking at Abbie who was being comforted by her sister Ella.

"Let's go find out." Falcon preceded them and pulled Abbie into a hug. "You okay, sweet pea?"

"I'm fine, Uncle Fal. He seemed like such a nice man when he came in, asking for books on the history of the Minster. I said he should wait and talk to you as history was one of your interests."

"It's okay. Turner, this is my niece and assistant Abbie. Abbie this is Detective Constable Bill Turner who wants to ask you some questions."

Abbie's face lit up as she met the young man and began answering his questions. Hugh winced as he'd bashed his arm, which was still sore from the bullet wound.

His back had also begun to hurt from being shoved into the doorway then onto the ground.

Ten minutes later, it was as though the incident had never happened. DC Turner had said he would keep an eye on the shop for the rest of the day and Abbie was happily making him a coffee in the staff kitchen.

"You're sure you don't want to go home?" Hugh heard Falcon ask her.

"I'm fine, Uncle Fal, don't fuss," she answered him then walked out and handed the coffee to Turner. She turned to them. "Why don't you two get some sleep? You both look dreadful. I'll be okay with Bill here."

Hugh hid his smile as Falcon growled. Pulling his lover after him, they left Abbie to it and made their way upstairs. They really needed to catch up with sleep before this

evening, but it didn't mean they couldn't have some fun as

well.

#

Falcon

In the early hours of the next morning, Falcon and Hugh joined the rest of his family in the sarcophagus room under the streets of York. They were ready to move Malik.

Francis, Hugh and Falcon had manhandled the dolly down the stairs and through the tunnels to the three rooms. They stood around, examining the sarcophagus and discussing the best way to move it to the dolly.

Once they had agreed, Francis lent his vampire strength to Falcon and Ollie and they carefully manoeuvered the heavy marble on to the dolly. Falcon and Ollie were out of breath by the end of it, but Francis didn't appear to be bothered by the exertion.

Falcon shook his head, remembering the first time he'd seen his father moving a heavy object.

#

It had not been that long since they'd been rescued from the facility, and they were setting up their bedrooms in the new house Francis had bought for them all to live in. Falcon's was all done so he was helping get Robin's sorted. Francis had a heavy armoire that would fit nicely into the room, and it was in the back of the moving truck.

"Give us a hand, Fal." Francis motioned for Falcon to follow him out to the driveway.

It was only when he dropped his end and Francis had

taken the weight of the whole, that Falcon realised just how strong his new father was. He hadn't needed his help; he had wanted to make Falcon feel wanted.

#

Now, he stood with Hugh and watched as Francis and Robin secured the sarcophagus to the dolly.

"Is there anything else we need from here?" Robin asked, standing up from where he'd been crouched next to the marble.

"How do you mean?" Hugh asked.

"After today, you're informing the police about this place. I can't see us being able to get down here freely for a while after that. I'm sure they'll be investigating how everything was here all this time without being discovered before."

"You're right, Rob." Falcon moved into the 'gentleman's club' room. "There are a couple of books I noticed the other day that I think we need to rescue. They may help with clues about what happened here. I meant to pick them up earlier and get Dad to go through them."

Francis and Robin moved from the inner room to join Falcon in front of the shelves on the wall.

"What books are those?" Francis asked him.

Falcon picked them up and showed them to his father. Francis nodded, then pointed to two more and Falcon reached for them. One of them appeared to be stuck, so he moved closer to examine it.

"Hugh, can you bring that light over here?" he asked, pointing to one of the battery powered arc lights they had scattered around the room.

Hugh brought the light and set it up so it was pointing

directly at the bookcase. "Look." He pointed to the shelf. It looked as though an old notebook had become stuck behind a hardback volume and pushed to the back.

Falcon reached forward and gently pulled at the book. The notebook was quite thick and appeared to have several pieces of paper slotted between various pages.

After a moment of carefully dislodging the other book, Falcon pulled the notebook carefully towards him and held it up for the others to see. He opened it to its fly cover and read out loud: "*Hispana Nonus* – John Jarratt, Legate 1873-1875."

"Now that will be very interesting," Francis remarked as he and Robin began to move the dolly down the first tunnel. "Bring it with you, Fal."

Falcon nodded. He was bringing it anyway as he couldn't wait to see what John Jarratt had recorded. He presumed 'Legate' meant he was in charge of the society at that time. With any luck it might mention what had happened with Malik and why they had targeted him.

Getting the sarcophagus down the tunnels on the dolly was harder than bringing the empty dolly in with them. Again, Francis's vampire strength came in useful when they got to the stairs up to the boiler room. They pulled the dolly up and then outside on to Oglethorpe Street. Fortunately, they didn't have that far to go before they got to the safe house in the close near to the Minster.

As they moved the dolly down the path behind the Minster, Falcon and Hugh kept a close eye out for anyone who might see them, but there weren't that many people out and about at 3am on an early Tuesday morning. Plus, Francis had cast a net around them that would hopefully stop people from seeing them. They'd stopped and held their breaths when three very drunk young men meandered past, but they never even noticed them, let alone the dolly.

Despite that, Falcon still felt on edge as the dolly created a racket as they steered it down the cobbled street. He drew in a shaky breath as they got to number 33 and opened the door. They were able to move the sarcophagus to the large airy back room, which had been set up like a hospital. There was a high bed with an IV stand ready and waiting, and all the equipment you could expect to find on an ICU ward was there for their use.

The next thing to do would be to open the sarcophagus and move Malik's sleeping body from there to the bed. That, however, could wait until later.

Francis would be staying at the house until Malik was ready to leave under his own steam. His bedroom had been set up upstairs and he thanked his sons and Hugh for their help and sent them all home to catch up on some sleep.

Holding hands, Falcon and Hugh made their way back towards Stonegate and the bookshop. It was 5 am and the streets were beginning to come alive as York began its day. The sun was beginning to rise and though it was still cold in the early morning air, it felt as though it was going to be another warm May day.

Stopping on Stonegate, Falcon pulled Hugh towards him and put his arms around the other man.

"Thank you."

Hugh smiled at him. "What are you thanking me for?"

"For being here with us this morning. For agreeing to wait to let the police know about the tunnels until Malik was safely out of the way. Just thank you..."

He pulled Hugh in for a possessive kiss, almost mauling his mouth, until he got the whimper he was after. Hugh pulled away to take a deep breath before diving back in again.

After a moment or two, Falcon pulled him into a hug. He could feel Hugh's arousal along with his own. "Come on. We're not far away, let's go to bed."

Hugh grinned at him, then allowed himself to be towed towards the bookshop and their bedroom above it.

#

It was midday before Falcon joined Abbie in the bookshop. He was feeling guilty after the previous day. He'd been neglecting the shop whilst he was busy with Hugh and his father. Feeling as though he needed to spend some more time there, he sent Abbie off for some lunch and began checking and replying to some of the shop's email.

About an hour later, Hugh joined him. After esquiring if there was anything he could do to help, he was given a hand-held reader and asked to check inventory.

Abbie returned from lunch and with her was the young officer from the day before, Bill Turner. They were laughing together as they entered the shop.

"Uncle Fal!" Abbie greeted him. "See who I met at the coffee shop?"

"Turner," Falcon greeted him.

"Just making sure Abbie's okay after yesterday," Turner replied, going red in the face.

"Aww isn't that sweet," Abbie gushed as she turned to relieve Hugh from his inventory duties.

"How are you doing, Mr McHughes?" Turner asked.

"Better than yesterday, thanks. Though I will have bruises upon bruises before long. Any news from yesterday?"

Turner nodded. "It's part of the reason I headed over this

way today. We interrogated Max Damson – the man we arrested here yesterday – and we're following up on some of the information he gave us. Especially around the kidnapping of Mr Summers from the hospital in Manchester."

"He was involved in that?" Falcon asked.

"He was. He admitted it when we agreed to certain conditions about his arrest." "In other words, you came to a deal."

Turner nodded. "We have. He also gave us a couple of addresses we didn't know about to check out."

"I don't suppose you're willing to share those with us?"

"Sorry. I would if I could. At the moment, DI Matlock hasn't given us permission to share that information."

"I'll phone her and see if she's willing to let us know. I need to speak to her anyway," Hugh said, coming over to Falcon and kissing him on the cheek. "I'll be upstairs talking to Deidre. Call me when it's time to head over to your dad's."

Chapter Twenty-Three

Hugh

After a very uncomfortable conversation with Deidre Matlock, Hugh had agreed to meet her and Jack Speight on Ogleforth and show them the tunnels and the rooms underneath. He'd agreed with Falcon that no mention would be made of Malik, just the task Father John had sent them on and what they had found in the 'gentleman's club' room.

"Good morning," he greeted Deidre and Jack as he approached them.

"Hugh." Jack grinned at him and held his hand out. "Feels like we're on a boys' own adventure!"

They laughed but Deidre frowned. "Why don't you show us what you found, McHughes?"

Ouch, she was still mad at him. He nodded and led the way to the boiler room at the back of the building, handing Deidre the key to the door. He didn't mention that it was a copy, letting her think it was the only one.

"Follow me," he said, leading the way down the stairs and to the door at the back.

He was glad there was no sign of their passing with the dolly last night; he didn't want to try and explain to them about the sarcophagus.

Francis and Robin had been in the previous evening to clear up and check that there was no sign that Malik's body had ever been there.

"We spent some time mapping the place," he explained as they walked. "We only had a rudimentary map that Father John gave us, which was sadly out of date, but we think we've got everything now and the only entrance left open is the one we came through."

"What made you close off the others?" Jack asked.

"Swales's goons kept finding their way in using the version of Father John's map he gave them when he was taken. Plus, we didn't want anyone else finding them accidentally."

When they reached the first room, Hugh reached out and switched on some of the arc lights, putting his torch down on the table. He turned to see the effect the reveal of the room was having on Matlock and Speight. They were staring around the room in astonishment.

"Wow," Matlock said as she spun slowly in place. This is..."

"Yeah," Hugh agreed. Though he'd become used to the room, he could still remember the first time he'd seen it.

"And you say it's an exact replica of what the York *Gentleman's Club* used to look like?" she asked.

"It is," Hugh replied. He pulled his phone from his pocket to show her the photograph they'd found of the club in the *York Explore* archives. The room was shown in all its glory in black and white. It was exactly the same, down to the type of decanter and glasses on the sideboard.

Hugh led them into what had been the sarcophagus room and showed them all the weapons that were on the wall, from Roman swords to the gatling guns.

"How many weapons are there?" Speight asked, already taking photos of the room.

"You know, I've never counted them," Hugh replied. "It looks like there's representation of weapons through the ages. As far as we've been able to ascertain, nothing has been added since the mid-19th century."

"Are there just the two rooms?" Matlock asked.

"There's one more, but we have to go back into a different tunnel to get to the outside door. The one that led into here from there has been covered over." He led them back out and around to the outer door. "When we first arrived, there were spell traps on the door. We had to clear those first before we could enter."

Matlock raised an eyebrow. Hugh knew from previous cases he'd worked on with her that she wasn't exactly a believer in magic and the paranormal, but he'd never let it stop him.

They entered the smaller room with its flagstone floor and stood in the middle of the room. As with every other time he'd been in here, he shivered as a feeling of fear and horror overcame him. He stepped outside with the excuse that there wasn't really enough room in there for three of them.

Jack joined him a moment later, looking uncomfortable. "Not a nice room."

"No," Hugh agreed as they waited for Matlock. "I don't even want to think about what might have taken place there."

A moment later Matlock joined them. "I've seen enough for now. Let's get back upstairs and I can contact the higher ups and see what they want to do about this. You say it was one of the Canons at the Minster that alerted you to this place first?"

"Yeah, Father John McKenzie. He was kidnapped and killed by Swales as well.

How Swales found out about this place I don't know. I remember when he showed up at the hospital he kept going on about treasure under the Minster, but..." He looked around them. "I guess some of those books and weapons could be considered treasure, though I'm not sure if that's what he was referring to."

"Hmpf." Matlock replied. She was still mad, not just about them keeping this news to themselves for a few weeks, but also for the fact that Francis had gone over her head yesterday and arranged for the addresses Turner had got out of Swales's henchman to be released to Falcon.

What she didn't know was that Raven, with Falcon along with him, was out there now, flying over the moors and looking for any sign of Gil at each of the addresses. Hugh hoped they had found him. He was concerned for his friend, especially as he still had a broken leg.

They reached Ogleforth and Matlock dismissed him. He knew she'd come back around; they'd worked with each other on several cases, and she'd never stayed mad at him for long. Checking his watch, he headed back to the shop. He'd assured Falcon he would keep an eye on Abbie whilst he was out with Raven.

#

There were several customers in the shop when Hugh got there and he jumped in to help Abbie serve by bagging up their purchases and running the card machine. Together they made quick work of the queue.

"I see you're popular this morning." He smiled at Abbie.

She laughed and hugged him. "We've been busy since the other day when the police were here. Many of them are just curious, but once they're here they have a look at the books and stock up. I've sold loads of those ghost tour books Falcon has in stock. You can always guarantee that ghosts sell in York."

"I heard there's a shop where you can buy your own ghost?"

"*York Ghost Merchants*. They're on St Saviourgate, so not that far away. You can get them by post as well," she replied.

Hugh laughed. Well, this was a tourist area. Whatever sold, he guessed. He'd never been on a ghost walk. Maybe when this was all over he could get Falcon to go on one with him.

The afternoon passed slowly, even though they were busy. Hugh worried about Falcon and Gil. He wished Fal would contact him and let him know how he was doing.

By closing time, he'd just finished serving a family from Northumberland who had all bought a book, from the parents down to the baby in the pram. He'd had a good chat with them about where they lived, sharing memories of the time he'd spent in Morpeth. Ushering them out of the shop, he turned the lock and was about to help Abbie cash up when his phone rang.

Quickly pulling it out of his pocket, he answered, "Fal?"

"We've found him, Hugh." Falcon sounded tired. "Can you get to Old Malton and bring Francis with you? Raven's phoning him now. I've also reached out to Matlock."

"I can do that. Is he okay? Did you see him?" "I did. We'll

know more when we get there."

#

Falcon

Falcon ended the call with Hugh and turned to Raven. They were both sitting outside of a café in the marketplace in Malton. It had been an exhausting day. Starting from 6 am, they'd been searching for Gil at the addresses passed on to them. They'd started in Whitby but didn't find anything there, so they'd driven to Old Malton and Raven had taken to the air once more. Accompanying him, Falcon had used their eyes to search the grounds of the large house near Old Malton. He'd left Raven to search the grounds, then 'spoke' to several local birds for their memories and to get them to fly closer to the house.

Following up an impression from one of the starlings, he'd got it to fly to an upstairs window. Looking in, he'd spotted Gil laid on a bed in the room. It was hard to tell if he was okay or not from the view he had. He'd left the bird to keep watch and let Raven know he could land and shift once more.

"Here you go." The young man who'd served them brought their coffees and a couple of pastries out to them.

"Thanks," Falcon said, glad they'd found somewhere still open in the early evening.

He slumped back in his chair, enjoying the coffee and the sweetness of the pastry.

They had about an hour before Hugh and Francis would be with them. He'd phoned DI Matlock and asked for the police to join them at the house at 7 pm. She'd sighed but agreed. It seemed her boss had overruled her and told her to work directly with Francis and his sons. She'd not been happy, but as she'd said, at least they were making progress.

"Penny for them?" Raven asked after they'd both been quiet for a few moments. "Not sure they're worth that much!"

Falcon grinned at his brother. "I was just wondering if I could get Hugh to go away with me for a few days after this is all over."

"Where had you in mind?"

"I'm not bothered. It would just be nice to be together, the two of us, with nothing life threatening going on."

"Anywhere with a bed then." Raven grinned at him and Falcon laughed. Yeah, that would do.

#

Just under an hour later, they were back at the house in Old Malton. It was a fairly new building and there were a couple of cars parked in the driveway. Just as they got out of their car, a local police vehicle drew up and DC Speight, along with DC Turner from York, got out with a uniformed PC.

"Falcon, Raven," Speight acknowledged, then introduced everyone. By this time, Hugh and Francis had arrived.

Fortunately, they'd agreed to meet out on the main road, so Falcon was hopeful that the inhabitants hadn't seen them yet. He stepped up to Hugh and squeezed his hand in greeting. He was rewarded with a smile just for him.

"Glad you could join us. I believe Gil is being held in one of the upstairs bedrooms at the back." Falcon knew exactly which one, but since neither Speight nor Turner knew about his abilities, he didn't want them to question how he knew.

"Shall we?" Speight asked and the uniformed officer who had been introduced as Mandy Smith strode towards the driveway.

They all followed behind as a police van with more uniformed officers drove up and blocked the driveway so anyone inside would not be able to get out. It might have been a bit of overkill, but they had no idea what they were dealing with.

Speight pounded his fist loudly against the wooden door. There was no answer, but Falcon could tell there was someone inside. It felt like they'd just upset an ant hill.

Several of the officers had gone round to the back, and there were shouts and scuffles as comments over the radio came back that some of the residents were making a run for it.

Speight turned to a couple of uniformed officers, who between them were carrying a small battering ram. Applying it to the door, they shouted, "Police!" And then entered the property.

There was no-one in immediate view, so Falcon and Hugh followed the police officers through to the kitchen area. It looked as though they'd disturbed the residents as they had been sitting down to dinner as there were five half eaten plates of food around the table.

A large glass wall looked out over the garden and Falcon could see that the police had several men corralled and were putting them in cuffs.

"Upstairs, you said?" Hugh asked Falcon.

"Yes, come on."

As they were making their way up the stairs, they could hear Gil's voice calling out. "Police? In here! Help!"

"We're coming, Gil. Hold on!" Hugh shouted back.

"Hugh?" Gil sounded relieved.

When they got to the right door, there was a key in the outside of the lock. Falcon turned it and gestured Hugh into the room. Gil was sitting down on the bed, his leg propped up as best as he could. He looked grim and in pain, and his face showed several bruises.

"Thank god," he said as they came in the room. "I was beginning to think no-one would find me."

"We're here now," Hugh said as he helped his friend get up from the bed. "Come on, let's get you out of here."

Between them Falcon and Hugh got Gil down the stairs to the front room. Matlock had now arrived, and she was talking to Francis, who was looking through a small, semi-familiar book.

"Mr Summers," Matlock greeted him. "It's good to see you, sir. There's a paramedic on his way to assess you."

Gil nodded as Hugh helped him sit on one of the sofas. Falcon walked over to his father, wondering what he was so fascinated by. "Dad?" he asked.

Francis held the book up, and Falcon saw that it was similar to the one he'd found in the underground room.

"Another journal?"

"Yes, from 1875. Look here." He pointed to a cut out of a newspaper article. "Excursion Train Struck by York Express: 10 people dead." Then he pointed to one of the names – John Jarratt was listed amongst the dead.

"Ah." Was all Falcon could think of to say. "That might explain a couple of things."

"What was that?" Matlock asked, stopping her conversation with Turner and Speight and turning to them.

"I was just saying that the men caught here today might be able to explain a couple of things about what's going on,"

Falcon replied.

"Ma'am?" One of the police officers interrupted and Matlock turned her attention to him. After a few moments, she sighed. "Thank you, Pollard." Matlock replied. "I want your report on my desk first thing in the morning."

"Yes Ma'am." Pollard confirmed before he left the room.

"It looks like we're a day late," reported Matlock. "Ian Swales was here yesterday according to Big Jimmy, one of the guys we took into custody. He was complaining about how Mr Byrde and his family were 'getting in his way' and it was time they 'put a stop to it'."

"Has anyone else said anything?" asked Hugh.

"Not yet. Just that one guy mouthing off. The rest are remaining quiet. We'll interrogate them when we get them back to the station. See what else they know."

Falcon turned around to check on Hugh and saw he was talking to Gil. The paramedic had arrived and was gently checking over Gil's face and closing a couple of cuts with butterfly bandages. He left Francis to talk to Matlock and went to join them.

"How are you doing, Gil?" he asked.

"Better than he could be," the paramedic answered for him.

"What he said." Gil looked up at him. "The leg is still okay, but it aches a lot as I've not had any painkillers and hardly any food or drink for a few days. Other than that, it's just bruising and a few cuts."

"There you go." The paramedic stood up. "That's all I can do for you. As I suggested earlier, you'll need to make an appointment with the fracture clinic to have your leg X-rayed and make sure it's definitely okay."

Gil nodded. They shook hands before the paramedic went

to give his report to DI Matlock.

"Here." Hugh handed Gil a bottle of water and some ibuprofen, along with a couple of cookies he'd scrounged from somewhere.

"What do you want to do, Gil?" He asked him a moment later. "You're welcome to come back to York with us."

"Thank you. I'd like that. Not that I can make the stairs in your place."

Hugh laughed. "I've given up the rental maisonette and have been staying with Fal. Imogen and Lucinda are safe in France."

"He can stay in the house with me," Francis said as he came up to them. "There's a room on the ground floor you can use."

"Sounds good," Gil replied. "So, what's been happening since I've been gone?"

Francis laughed. "We'll catch you up in the car. It looks like the police are going to be here for a while yet, looking for clues as to where Swales may have gone. There's also a chance that he might come back, so they're going to leave someone here to keep an eye on the place."

"Let's head back then," Falcon said, helping Hugh get Gil up from the sofa. Francis went off to tell Matlock they were going, and the others made their way out to Falcon's car.

Chapter Twenty-Four

Hugh

After getting Gil settled in the safe house near the Minster, Hugh and Falcon had retreated to the shop. Hugh had picked up the journal Francis had found at the house in Old Malton and was reading through it the following morning.

#

The old man was right. I knew it had to be when the goddess had led me to him. Though it took several days to excavate the entrance, we were finally able to see where the Mithraeum where the Ninth worshiped whilst in Eboracum.

I have left instructions with my Centurions to make the place sound and to replicate the pleasing surroundings of our club in York under the city. Once set up I will seek out an Old One and we can complete our mission of returning the Eagle to its rightful place.

#

* * *

"This guy was certifiable," Hugh remarked to Falcon after reading the last piece aloud to him.

"He certainly seemed to be following several old Roman gods and goddesses. It was well known that Roman soldiers worshipped both Mars and Mithras, with the latter meeting in underground meeting rooms. I wonder about the reference to the Eagle?"

"The Eagle of the Ninth, you mean?" Hugh gestured at the Rosemary Sutcliffe book that Falcon was flicking through.

"It's been a while since I read this." He smiled. "I remember rooting for Marcus to find his father's final resting place and recover the Eagle."

"I read it in school," Hugh replied. Falcon handed him the book and he skimmed through it. "It was written long after Jarratt wrote about it in this journal though."

"There's nothing in the journal Dad found in the underground library about it. It speaks of treasure relating to the Ninth Legion, but that's it."

"The same treasure Swales is interested in finding?"

"If he had this journal, then yes, it's likely. The question remains is where did Swales get this from? Until earlier this year he was still incarcerated in a secure mental institution."

"I'll get Gil to phone the owner of the institution and see if anyone can remember it being in Swales's possession whilst he was there. The only thing I can think of is he got it from one of the other residents."

"Maybe. Or a member of staff. Gil will be glad of something to do, other than stare at the four walls of his room."

Hugh laughed. Gil was an active man like himself and even a couple of days of inactivity had begun to unsettle him. They'd agreed that until Swales was captured it was not a good idea for him to be out and about. Hugh and Falcon themselves were being extra careful anytime they were outside in the city. A plainclothes policeman was always around the arcade now, in case Swales came there. Hugh wasn't sure how desperate the man was, but surely after losing Gil and the house in Old Malton, he must be getting worried.

Falcon's phone buzzed and he pulled it out of his pocket to check the text. He held it up to show Hugh. "Dad says they're ready to go ahead and wake Malik."

"I guess we'd better get over there then."

#

Hugh wasn't sure that the bright, hospital-like room they'd set up for Malik leant itself to a high-level magical working. For some reason he always associated workings with dark rooms and men in hoods. He knew that was his own imagination overriding good sense and smiled at himself for his whimsy.

Francis was at the foot of the bed with his sons and Hugh arranged around it, along with Gil, who didn't have much of a gift but had wanted to be involved. They were all waiting for Francis's instructions.

Robin was at the head near where an IV stand had been set up. He'd just finished inserting a needle into Malik's inert left arm and blood had already begun to drip through. Francis hoped that this would avoid any possibility of Malik attacking anyone should he wake thirsty.

"Ready," Robin told his father and stepped back to join hands with Ollie, resting his left hand on Malik's forehead. Around the bed they all joined hands and Pip, who was opposite Robin, put his hand on Malik's chest. The circle was complete.

"*Excita nunc! Surge, surge, surge! Surge et iterum vivere!*" Francis spoke the words of the spell and imposed his vampire magic upon them. They all then joined Francis in saying the spell, and Hugh felt the power run through him and all around the circle, going from man to man. Robin gasped as it ran though his hand to Malik's head and Pip gasped as it flowed into Malik's heart.

"You can release each other now," Francis said, stepping forward. He moved to the head of the bed and rested his forehead upon Malik's. A moment later he smiled."

"I believe it has worked," he announced. "Now we just have to wait for him to wake up properly."

"How long will that take?" Robin asked, looking down at the vampire on the bed. "A few days, maybe," Francis replied. "Hopefully no more than that."

Hugh and the others filed out of the room and entered the kitchen dining room that overlooked the small back yard. French doors led out on to the patio.

"Does anyone else feel as though that was a bit underwhelming?" Ollie asked.

"A bit," Pip said, sitting at the table. "But something definitely worked as I felt the power surge there at the end."

"I hope he can throw some light on what Jarratt was trying to achieve," Falcon said, as he handed Hugh a cup of coffee. "He's the only one who met the man."

"Andrew never met him?" Hugh asked.

"No. He only ever went to the club twice with a couple of the other members of Lady Emma's coterie and Jarratt was not present either time."

"You've spoken to him?"

"I phoned him and Percy about the journal the other day. They did a bit of looking up for me and found Jarratt's death certificate, as well as those of some other people who died in the crash. It seems the express train was returning from Edinburgh."

"I wonder what they were doing in Scotland?"

"Looking for the lost legion?" Falcon posited. "Most people still believe the Ninth was lost in North Britain, or Scotland as we know it, as in the Rosemary Sutcliffe book. Even though opinion is now divided between Scotland and Germany for their last resting place."

Francis came into the room and sat wearily down at the table. Without saying a word, Falcon leaned over to the fridge and pulled out a blood bag for his father. Francis smiled his thanks at him before piercing the bag with his fangs and gulping it all down.

Hugh watched, still fascinated by Francis's need for blood. Falcon had told him that he rarely drank blood directly from the source – another person. Instead, he relied on blood bags for his everyday nutrition.

"Where do we go from here?" Gil asked.

"I'm not sure," Hugh answered him. "I'm still waiting to hear from Matlock and whether they got any more information after arresting Swales's men in Old Malton."

"I don't think it will be long before Swales makes his move," Francis said, now getting a glass of water, having disposed of the empty blood bag.

"I agree," Falcon spoke up. "He's desperate now. Whatever he wants, or thinks he wants, I'm sure he'll strike soon."

Hugh sighed. He just wished this was all over one way or another. A strange mission that had gone from watching Falcon Byrde and his mysterious comings and goings had turned to him falling for said man. He wanted some time to concentrate on them, without some mad man trying to destroy them in his quest for an unknown treasure.

#

Malik

Malik couldn't tell how much time had passed since the last time his consciousness had floated to the top. He lay there, inert, passive. There was nothing he could do to change his situation. All he could do was rail at the men who had put him there.

He sensed that there was movement in the room and several voices. He was sure he recognised one of the voices, but he wasn't able to confirm that. Then, for the first time in what felt like forever, he felt movement. Was he being moved? What was happening?

#

There was a strange beeping noise. It made its way through his consciousness and began to annoy him. He'd never heard that before. As he listened, he realised that there were other new noises. He struggled to understand what was happening, but the lethargy was too much for him. He went under once more.

#

The noise was back. There was also the sound of voices. He listened; he could hear them more sharply than he'd ever been able to.

"How's he doing?" A voice he didn't recognise asked someone else in the room.

"Better than I thought." That voice again! Louder, clearer. The name that belonged to that voice was almost on the tip of his tongue. He listened again, realising he'd lost some of the conversation.

"... how much longer?"

"Hopefully not too long now. I've got an IV going for blood transfusion, and so long as it's kept full, there shouldn't be any problems with thirst when he wakes."

"That's good." This voice was male and young. The other male was older and someone he knew. Had he finally been rescued? Oh gods, please say he'd been rescued.

#

The beeping noise had stopped, though there were still other mechanical noises in the background. Malik felt his senses beginning to come back. First, he realised that he was laying on a soft mattress, with cool sheets and a comfy pillow. Not anything like he remembered.

Then slowly, oh so achingly slowly, he managed to raise his eyelids and see for the first time in however long it had been since he was trapped. He closed them quickly. The room was bathed in white bright light.

He opened them again and looked around him. He didn't recognise anything, not the room, the bed, or any of the strange machinery.

He coughed then, surprising himself. He jerked upwards, before falling back onto the comfortable mattress once more. He tried sitting up but couldn't find the strength to do so.

The door opened and a young man with short blond hair

entered the room and walked towards him. There was something off about his gait, but Malik couldn't work out what it was.

"You're awake!" The young man smiled at him, before returning to the door and shouting for someone called Francis.

"It's okay," he announced, coming back towards the bed. "You'll be alright. It's just…" He hesitated. "Well, let's just say you've been asleep for quite some time. Lots of things have changed."

Malik just looked at him. He was gorgeous and his striking blue eyes stared at him, before he moved around the bed to adjust something just outside his sight.

The door opened again and another man came in. Xisco! He looked upon his old friend and he could feel water beginning to leak from his eyes. He was weeping.

Xisco. Or what was it the young man had called him? Francis, that was it. Francis came up to the bed and took his hand.

"It's good to have you back with us, Mal," he said, squeezing his hand tightly.

There were tears in his eyes as well.

"I've changed the blood bag, Dad." The younger man spoke

"Thank you, Robin. Malik this is my youngest son, Robin. He has been helping me with your care for the last couple of days since we were able to disperse the spell you had on you."

Malik winced then opened his mouth to try and talk. All that came out was a sort of grunt.

"Here." Robin was there immediately with a cup of water. Malik sipped it carefully. His throat was parched, and he was amazed he wasn't desperate for blood.

"It will take time for you to heal properly," Francis said, as he went around the room checking a few things.

"How... how did you find me?" he whispered.

"By accident."

"What?"

"One of my sons, acting on behalf of a client, found some tunnels under the city, then eventually discovered three rooms. A room that looked like it came from an old gentleman's club, an empty room with flagstones on the floor, and a third room with many weapons on the wall and a black sarcophagus in the centre. You were in the sarcophagus."

Malik was astonished. He remembered then the room that Jarratt had taken him to. The strange likeness to the York *Gentleman's Club*. Then the cold of the flagstone floor where they stood around him and put him into the sleep that Xi... Francis had just woken him from.

"Why aren't I thirsty?" he managed to get out.

"We've been giving you blood intravenously for the last few days. I am glad to see that my theory that it would counter the thirst has proven sound." Francis smiled at him. "A lot has happened since you were last in the world, my friend. More wars, of course. When aren't there? But the machinery, the technology. Man has learned to fly machines. Medicine has come on leaps and bounds."

Malik listened to him, fascinated by what he had to say. But he could feel his eyelids getting heavier again.

"Sleep," the young man Robin said. "We'll be here when you wake. Ask any questions and we'll try and answer you as best we can."

Malik opened his mouth to ask a question but nothing came out and he gave into sleep once more.

* * *

#

Falcon

Nothing much seemed to happen over the next few days. Matlock reported back that they were following up a few leads, but none of them sounded promising. Swales had gone to ground again.

The only piece of positive news from the police was that the security guard who had been missing after the last break in at the agency's offices had been found alive.

He'd been hiding out at his sister's and had been arrested for assisting in a robbery. So far, he claimed he didn't know who the perpetrators were, just that he'd been paid a good sum of money to ignore the robbery in progress. It seems he'd had a rather large gambling debt.

Falcon and Hugh were heading back to the safe house near the Minster. They were taking a round-about route, as Falcon didn't trust Swales not to have them under observation. Confident that they weren't being followed, they knocked on the door of the house in the quiet area.

Robin answered the door and grinned at his big brother. "Malik is awake," he announced, letting them in.

"That's great." Falcon smiled back at him, squeezing his shoulder on the way by. "Dad's waiting for you in his room."

They headed towards the room at the back of the house and were pleasantly surprised to see the other vampire sitting up in bed looking a lot healthier than he had when they'd moved him from the sarcophagus.

Falcon approached the bed and stuck his hand out. "It's so good to see you awake and looking healthy."

"Thank you," Malik replied, as Hugh also leaned in and shook his hand.

"This is my eldest son Falcon and his partner Hugh," Francis introduced them. "It's good to meet more of my old friend's family," Malik acknowledged. "Though it's strange for me to see him with sons of his own, when he was a loner for such a long time."

"You've known each other a long time, haven't you?" Robin broke in as he entered the room followed by Gil, who was doing better and only using one crutch.

"Almost since the beginning," Malik said. "I am just so glad that Francis recognised me when you found me and agreed to help wake me. I'm still having difficulty in accepting that it's been over a century since I was last awake."

"I can imagine how disconcerting that must be for you. Especially given how many changes there have been since the 1870s." Falcon took a seat near the head of the bed.

"Yes. For many long years, not much seemed to change. Machinery was being slowly introduced and progress was slow for many centuries. It appears it has speeded up in the last 150 years."

"Considerably," Francis said. "It's been a wild time to live through. But you'll catch up, old friend."

Malik nodded and indicated the tablet laying on the bed. "Robin has begun showing me some of the wondrous things that have happened, using this magical seeing device."

Falcon grinned as he picked up the tablet and saw it was open at a video of the moon landing. Well, that was one place to start, he guessed.

"Malik, I'm sorry to have to ask you what happened all those years ago, but we need to know what Jarratt was after.

Why he kidnapped you and put you to sleep."

Malik's forehead creased as he contemplated Falcon's question. "It was strange," he began. "I had come across the antiquarian, Gilead Summerbell a few times before and he'd introduced me to Jarratt. A few nights later when I entered the club, I was told they were waiting for me in a private parlour upstairs. Curious as to what they could want, I joined them and accepted a drink. Summerbell left at that point, but he'd appeared nervous. I never saw him again."

"One of our friends found out he was arrested and jailed for a homosexual act.

Shortly after he was released, he died at his house in Woodmansey," said Falcon.

"I see. Poor man. And Jarratt?"

"Died in a train crash not long after you were trapped underground."

"Well, there's some justice there." Malik sighed. "I don't remember too much about what happened next. I'd been knocked unconscious and given some vile drink that put me out completely. I do remember Jarratt speaking about using my vampire energies to search for something in the past. How he was going to use me to enhance his own power and see into the past to find something that was lost. I admit by that time I'd stopped listening to him as I was very listless from the drug they'd given me. I came to once more when I was lying naked on a flagstone floor with several hooded men around me."

"Jarratt was putting the spell on you?" Hugh asked.

"I believe it must have been. After that, I floated in and out of consciousness. Occasionally I'd hear noises around me, but never too much to work anything out. I believe I heard your voice, old friend." He turned to Francis. "Then I woke up here."

"Thank you." Falcon pulled the small journal he'd been looking at the day before from his pocket and held it out so Malik could see the title. He looked confused.

"From our research we've discovered that Jarratt led a secret society who were very popular in the 18th and 19th centuries. It was based on the Roman Legion, the Ninth to be precise. The room we found you in had weapons from every period of history, but a lot of them were Roman. He appears to have inherited the society from someone he only ever refers to as the Old Man and named it *Hispana Nonus*."

"Ninth Spain," Malik muttered.

"Reading through this, it appears as though Jarratt had fixated on the Ninth Legion and thought he could reach through time by using you as some kind of battery. Storing your energy up until they needed it."

Malik shook his head. "What was he looking for? Do you know?"

"I think I might have an inkling. From what I can work out from his ramblings, he believed that the Ninth had excavated the rooms and tunnels under York and used them as a place to worship Mithras. He believed that they had some kind of magical powers that was imbued in their standard. The Eagle, if you like. Jarratt's aim was to reach back in time to find where the Eagle was abandoned after the Ninth's defeat in Scotland, he believed, and then set out to recover it. It may have been why he was on a train returning to York from Edinburgh when he was killed in the crash."

"He wanted the Eagle from the Ninth Roman Legion? That is what he wanted me for?" Malik looked stunned, then somewhat amused, and Falcon was nonplussed as to why.

"I believe so, yes. It's also what the man we are searching

for, Swales, is after. I believe Francis has filled you in on..." Falcon stopped talking as Malik began chuckling to himself. Before long, he was full-on laughing.

They all turned to look at the other vampire in astonishment. Not knowing what was going on, there were a few smiles on faces as people were affected by the hearty guffawing coming from Malik.

"He... he should..." He tried to get out some words but hadn't calmed down enough yet. After a moment, he picked up his glass of water, took a sip and tried again.

"It's ironic, and not really all that funny," he finally said, putting the glass back down. "All he had to do was ask. I could have told him where it was."

"What!" Falcon exclaimed as everyone started talking at once.

"Let him finish," Francis said, looking at his old friend and smiling.

"I have it. I have the Eagle of the Ninth but we both served in the Roman Army several times. I was attached to the Ninth in 110 AD when they were sent to the Rhine. I went with them as I had connections in the area.

"They had been in North Britain after they left Eboracum, but not for long before they were transferred out again. I wasn't present at their last stand. I had been sent to parley with a local petty prince, and when I returned a week later, all around the camp were dead bodies. I found no-one living. If anyone had survived, they had left before I got back. I found the Eagle hidden beneath the body of Marcellus its acquilifer, or standard bearer. It was in Germania, a very long time ago. I took it with me with the intention of returning it to Rome..." He faltered slightly. "Long story for a different day."

The room had quieted down whilst Malik was talking, and Falcon just stared at the vampire in disbelief. All this time. All this time, and the treasure Jarratt sought had been under his nose. If only he'd thought to talk to Malik first, things may have been different.

"I wouldn't have given it to him, of course," Malik said. "But I could have set him straight about it and it's paranormal powers."

Chapter Twenty-Five

Hugh

Hugh had been antsy since they'd talked to Malik the previous day. There was nothing he could do, and he hated waiting. Matlock had gone quiet on him again, and not even Francis could get her to open up. He could only assume she was following some leads and would get back to them once she knew some more information.

In the meantime, Hugh was killing time working in the bookshop with Abbie and Falcon. They'd been arguing over traditional publishing versus self-publishing all morning. He was in favour, Falcon not so much. He made headway though when Falcon agreed that given how large of a phenomenon it had become in the 2020s, stocking some books by self-published authors would probably be worth it. Hugh would take any victory he could get.

Taking his phone from his pocket, he pulled up the text string with Imogen.

How's the weather today?

* * *

He watched the three little dots whilst waiting for her answer. There were no customers in the shop and Abbie was making coffee for them.

Gorgeous!

You and Luci okay?

It was the same question he asked her every day and as usual the reply came back that they were both fine, giving him some description of what they'd done yesterday and their plans for the rest of the day. Imogen then asked a question.

Have you heard anything about our jobs?

It was the question Hugh had been anticipating for days now. He still wasn't sure how to answer her, but he wanted to let her know about Francis's offer that they go work for him.

Nothing solid yet. Looks like we'll be let go though. Francis has offered alternative employment.

A moment after, the phone rang in his hand with an incoming call.

"Imogen," he answered.

"What kind of alternative employment?"

He grinned. He knew she'd be interested. "Working for his paranormal investigation business. He's expanding and wants more researchers and field agents."

"Sounds interesting."

"Agreed. He's offered to take on myself, you and Gil. He said he'd even provide us with an office here in York. It would mean moving from Manchester, or commuting."

"I'd rather move," she replied, and Hugh could hear in her voice that she was seriously considering the opportunity. "What about Gil?"

"He's all in. Personally, I think he was getting a little bored at Swales's Agency and is looking for a new path."

"How is he?" she asked next.

"Doing well. Why don't you phone him? I know he's at that stage where he's frustrated with not being able to get about okay. I'm sure he'd love to chat to you."

"I'll call him next. Any idea when I can come home?"

"I still don't know. Things might be coming to a head soon. I'll let you know as soon as I do."

They spoke for a few moments longer on general day to day activities before Imogen hung up to call Gil.

#

"Hey?"

Hugh looked round. Falcon was standing in the doorway that led to his study, leaning on the door jamb. He smiled at his lover.

"Hey yourself," he replied, moving over to him.

"So..." Falcon began, then hesitated. "I overheard you talking to Imogen about the job Dad's offered. Are you seriously thinking about taking it?"

Hugh leaned into Falcon's personal space and pressed a kiss to his lips, before pulling back and nodding.

"I am. Gil as well. I think Imogen will be on board too. I'll have to sell my flat in Manchester, but that shouldn't be a problem. I can rent here until I get settled."

Falcon's hands came to rest on Hugh's hips as he pulled him in for another leisurely kiss. A giggle from Abbie from the front of the shop reminded them that they weren't alone. Reluctantly, Hugh pulled back from Falcon.

"You like that idea?"

"You know I do," Falcon responded, straightening up. "I'd much prefer you being in York than Manchester when this is all over."

"So would I," Hugh agreed, smiling at him. "And in case you were wondering, yes, I am all in with this relationship. I want to be with you, Falcon."

The bell above the door tinkled. Hugh drew in a breath and turned round, only to find DI Matlock and DC Speight coming in. Hugh hoped they had good news to share.

"Jack, Deidre," he said, coming forward to greet them, with Falcon following on behind. "Say you've got some good news for us."

Matlock grimaced. "Not good as such but news, nonetheless. We found out where Ian Swales has been holing up and have been keeping an eye on it. So far, he's not returned there. We did, however, apprehend Virginia Swales, Robert's wife. She was dropping off some groceries, so we're pretty confident he's still using the place."

"Did she have anything useful to say?" Hugh asked. "Hang on a minute, I thought you were still holding her over Robert's situation?"

"We were. She got out on bail. It seems Ian has persuaded her to look after him. He promised her untold riches and that if she divorced Robert, he'd marry her."

Hugh could only look at Matlock as she told him this. He'd met Virginia only once or twice and he'd always thought of her as shallow and what his mother had called 'high maintenance'. That she'd divorce Robert for his twin didn't surprise him at all.

"We've been keeping her under surveillance," Jack said. "When the officer tailing her yesterday realised the direction she was going in, he alerted myself and DI Matlock. We were able to get to the address not long after she did. She was… surprised to see us there. I don't think she thought we'd still be looking for Ian."

"She's cooperating with you?" Hugh asked.

"Hmm," Matlock hummed. "A bit. Her solicitor has told her that she needs to be as open with us as possible – she at least understands the nature of the trouble Mrs Swales is in."

"What's the plan?"

"We're monitoring the situation all the time," Matlock replied as she looked around the bookshop, her eyes roving over the shelves. "He's bound to show up at some point and when he does, we'll be ready for him. We have officers watching this new address, the entrance to those tunnels you showed us, this arcade and a few other places we know he frequented."

"You'll let us know?" Falcon asked. "When we have him, yes."

"Not before?" asked Hugh.

"Hugh," Jack answered. "We'll let you know as soon as we can, okay? I know you want to be getting on with your lives without this hanging over you, and so do we. But we need to follow procedure."

Hugh grunted. "Yeah, I know. It's just frustrating. I'm used to being more involved."

"I know." For the first time in a while, DI Matlock smiled at him. "To which end, I'm here to inform you that we've cleared the rooms under the city and the tunnels. You said you were going to catalogue the books and talk to the local archaeology people about the site and what to do with it going forward?"

"Francis has contacts," Falcon spoke up. "He intends to approach them in the next couple of weeks, or as soon as Ian is apprehended anyway. He believes there'll be a lot of interest in the place."

"I agree," Matlock replied. Indicating to Speight that they were finished, she headed for the door. "Keep us informed if you see or hear anything about Ian."

"We will. And Deidre? Thank you," said Hugh.

She gave a little wave and she and Jack left the shop.

#

Falcon

Falcon was hopeful after speaking to Hugh that afternoon that he would be staying in York. Maybe even staying with him? Or was he getting too far ahead of himself? He could see the two of them living and working together, both in the shop and for Francis.

He knocked on the door to Francis's safe house and once again Robin let them in. "Hi, bro. Hugh," Robin said as he let them through. "Everyone's in the lounge."

"Including Malik?" Falcon asked.

"Yep, he's fine to get up and move around. He... he has a few questions for you about the rooms. I told him I'd only been there a couple of times, but that you both had a lot more knowledge of them."

"Hugh," Gil greeted his friend first and started to rise one of the burgundy sofas. "Falcon, good to see you too."

"No, don't get up." Hugh pushed his friend back onto the sofa and joined him. Francis walked in the room and began passing the coffee he'd just made around.

Knowing everyone's preferences made it easier. He quietly handed Malik a blood bag and Falcon was glad to see him free from the IV.

"How are you feeling, Malik? It's good to see you up and about."

"I am well, thank you," Malik replied. "Did your brother tell you I have some questions for you?"

"He did, yes."

Falcon settled himself on the chair next to where Malik was sitting and sipped his coffee as he scrutinised the vampire. He still looked pale and a bit emaciated, though he was a lot better than he had been when they'd found him in the sarcophagus. Malik now held up John Jarratt's journals, one of which Falcon had read, the other not.

"Reading through these has been a troubling experience," Malik began. "I am still trying to accept what happened. I apologise for my hysterical outburst the other evening, but I cannot believe that the Eagle standard from the Ninth is what this has all been about."

"Don't worry about it. I can see why that would have struck you as extremely funny under the circumstances. Many men like Jarratt got involved with secret societies and thought they were invincible. His search for the Eagle was purely selfish and he wanted you to power that search. He must have had at least some inkling of magic or paranormal power to believe he could find the Eagle. The fact that he was traveling from Scotland only proves he didn't have enough of a clue as to where the Eagle actually was."

"Precisely," Malik answered as Robin sat down next to him on the sofa and handed him a drink, after taking the blood bag away.

Malik smiled at the younger man. Falcon watched their interaction for a few moments. *Interesting*, he thought. In the background, he could hear that Gil and Hugh were talking to Francis about his job offer. It sounded as though they were hammering out the practicalities. He turned his attention back to Malik.

"I am interested in seeing the room I was held captive in for all those years. Francis tells me that the authorities have released it?"

"Indeed they have. I spoke to Detective Inspector Matlock this afternoon and she has left it in our hands for the moment."

"I find it fascinating that women are now in positions of power. A complete change from the last few thousand years."

"Everything changes," Falcon agreed, wondering what it must be like for Malik. Not only had technology and machinery changed, but so too had society. Seeing it from his point of view would be difficult. He made a mental note to ask Andrew if he would talk to Malik. He was one person who could sympathise.

"Would you take me into the tunnels?"

"You really want to go?"

"I do. I have begun learning about this new world I find myself in. Your brother has been very helpful with this, but I find… I find that I need to put this chapter of my life to one side before I can move on to the next."

Francis joined them then, his hand on Falcon's shoulder. "You have to congratulate me, boy, your friends have agreed to join us." He gestured to Hugh and Gil across the room. "Meet your new colleagues."

Falcon grinned. He had been almost sure that Hugh would agree, and he was more than pleased at the opportunity to work with his lover and his colleague.

"That's brilliant news!" he exclaimed, getting up to shake Gil's hand before pulling Hugh into a crushing embrace. "Welcome aboard. What about Imogen?"

"I'll speak to her again in the morning," Gil answered, smiling at the room in general. "But when I spoke to her this afternoon, she was very keen on the idea. I don't think it will be an issue."

Everyone offered their congratulations, and they settled down once more. Inevitably, the discussion turned to Ian Swales and his strange insistence that Hugh should have killed Falcon when they first met. They'd put it down to his mental instability, but it still bothered them all. What was it about Falcon that had Swales wishing to kill him?

Falcon passed on Malik's request to visit the tunnels and the rooms where he had been held. After more discussion, it was agreed that Francis and Malik would accompany Falcon and Hugh to the tunnels the next day. They would still be wary and keep a weather eye out for Ian, or anyone acting suspicious.

No-one was sure how many men and women Ian had had working for him. He could now be on his own, or still have some lackeys left. Falcon was of the opinion that he was on his own, but Hugh wasn't sure.

"We'll drop by and pick you up here in the early afternoon," Falcon said to Malik. "We'll try to keep the route to the quieter areas. I'm not sure what you know about the changes to the city's infrastructure yet but traffic, for one, could be an issue. No more horses and carts, my friend."

Malik grimaced. "I have seen from the windows some of the machines you call cars and trucks. They are noisy and smelly and look unnatural to me. Though I am given to understand that they travel as fast, if not faster, than trains."

"Some do, yes. But there are speed limits and laws that have to be followed. And unlike trains, they do not have to stick to rails."

"So it would seem," Malik agreed. "I have this seeing box that Robin has given me. He said he could show me some moving pictures of modern-day York. I will watch them before tomorrow."

Falcon could only nod. Seeing the current city and experiencing it would be too very different things. However, he had to accept that a vampire who'd been alive for nearly three thousand years had to be able to adapt to changing times, else they would not have survived this long.

"You're getting tired," Robin spoke up from the other side of Malik. "Perhaps it's time to retire. We can watch the videos in the morning. I'll come just before lunch."

"Thank you, Robin. You are right. I should retire for the evening."

Everyone got up and began moving around in preparation for leaving. "Are you walking with us, Rob?" Falcon asked his little brother.

"I'm going to say a little while longer. It's okay, Fal, Dad will walk me home."

Falcon could only nod as he and Hugh said goodbye to the others. He could see that Robin was developing a crush on Malik. He hoped he wouldn't be too hurt when the vampire decided it was time to move on.

Chapter Twenty-Six

Hugh

Hugh had an uneasy feeling as they entered the tunnels from the entrance in Ogleforth. They had agreed with the police that they would only use that entrance as the others had been closed off to deter Ian and anyone else accessing them. It was early on Saturday afternoon and the uneasy feeling had been with him all morning. He didn't know the cause; he just knew something was going to happen. He'd spent a lot of time looking around that morning to make sure they weren't being followed, but he hadn't seen anyone that looked suspicious.

He reminded himself that there were two powerful vampires with them and that he and Falcon were not without their own skills. He watched as Malik descended the stairs that led from the boiler room to the tunnels. Malik had appeared to take in his stride the traffic around the Minster as they walked over to Ogleforth. But Hugh had seen him jump nearly out of his skin when a car had hooted its horn at some idiot tourist standing in the middle of the road trying to get a photo of the Minster.

Malik had been surprised at how much of York had remained the same since he was last awake. Obviously, they had explained that were new parts of the city, and Robin had shown him maps and photos. But still, the area around the Minster and the Minster itself hadn't changed that much.

"Watch the steps."

Hugh heard Falcon behind him, reminding him to keep his mind on what he was doing right now.

Reaching the tunnel, he flipped the switch that had been installed by the police, that lit up a string of electric lights. The area looked a lot less spooky now than it had when they first came this way.

"This is very strange," Malik remarked. "I have no memory of this part. I was unconscious when they brought me here."

"The first time Robin and I entered the tunnels," Falcon began, "we came in through an entrance that we've now closed off. The tunnel there was unstable, and I ended up twisting my ankle."

"I remember that." Hugh smiled. "I was sitting in the café when you came by."

"Having said that," Falcon continued, ignoring Hugh's remark, "we've tried to make this entrance as safe as possible. The other main entrance is from the Minster, but that has been blocked off by the staff there for the moment."

"How many entrances were there?" Malik asked.

"We're not sure how many there were originally but we found at least five. Though some of those were hardly passable now due to new buildings around them and drains being filled in. We're still not sure of the age of these tunnels. I think Jarratt was convinced they went back to the Roman

Eboracum or maybe the Viking Jorvik."

"They weren't here when I first visited Eboracum in the 1st century AD." Malik stretched his hand overhead and felt the ceiling of the tunnel. "The cut marks here are reminiscent of some Roman tunneling I have come across in the past. But it is hard to say for sure."

"Which is one of the reasons I want the archaeology department to investigate the area," Francis put in. "They have staff members who have a lot of experience with Roman archaeology."

They came to the end of the tunnels and stopped in front of the first door. The one that led into the 'gentleman's club' room. Hugh, who was leading the small group, leant forward and opened the door. Behind him he could hear Falcon explaining to Malik about the spell traps they'd originally found on the doors. He was of the opinion that they had been laid down by Jarratt to stop anyone from entering whilst he and his cohorts weren't there.

Hugh entered the room first and looked around. He could see signs that the police had been there, but nothing appeared to be out of place. He turned around when he heard Malik gasp.

"It's just as I remember." He turned in place, taking it all in. "An exact replica of the York *Gentlemen's Club* over near the river. Amazing. How much work this must have taken."

He wandered off to look at the books on the library wall, but Hugh could tell he wasn't unaffected by the room. The last time he'd been there he'd been held captive.

"Are you doing alright?" he asked the vampire.

"I… I'm overwhelmed," Malik admitted after a moment or two. "I remember the place as though it was yesterday, which in some sense it was for me."

Hugh left Malik to his thoughts and watched as the vampire ran his fingers over the back of one of the wingback chairs. Falcon had his phone out and was continuing to photograph the books so he could add them to the catalogue he was compiling. Francis had disappeared into the other room and Hugh followed him.

The room where the sarcophagus had been looked strangely different from the last time they had been in it. The plinth that it had sat upon looked forlorn without the decorated black marble on it. The walls, however, were still covered in the weapons from all ages. Francis was examining them.

"These belong in a museum," Hugh said as he joined the vampire near the weapons.

"They do. Hopefully that is what will happen to them. Maybe this will become a museum itself."

Hugh nodded. He was just about to join the others when he heard a whisper of a sound that shouldn't be there. He stopped, listening. It sounded as though someone was shuffling their feet and it was coming from the room that had the flagstone floor. He raised his eyebrow at Francis as he pointed towards the other room. Francis closed his eyes a moment, before opening them and mouthing 'someone's in there'.

Malik entered the room just then and shuddered. "This is where I was kept?" he asked.

"It was," Francis answered, as he gestured for them to be quiet. He whispered their concerns about the next room to Malik and gestured for them to return to the club room.

Falcon was still photographing books and looked up when they entered. Hugh held his finger to his lips, letting his lover know not to say anything. Falcon put the book he'd been looking at down and joined them.

"What do you think?" Francis whispered, stopping as a shadow fell into the room from the tunnel outside.

Ian Swales stepped nonchalantly into the room. He was holding a gun. He was not alone. Tucked against his side, with a gun to his head, was Robin.

They all started forward and Hugh could swear his heard hisses from Malik and Francis. He wanted to move, but was worried about upsetting Swales and causing him to hurt Robin.

"Finally," Swales began. "I was beginning to think none of you would show up. I was just about to follow you when this youngster turned up. Good timing."

Swales grinned and Hugh could see that instability in his eyes. He looked at Robin who was defiant and glaring at Swales.

"Ian," Hugh acknowledged the other man as he subtly moved to stand in front of Falcon and the others.

"McHughes. Still hanging around with these losers, I see. You should have stayed with my agency."

"The agency was never yours Ian, it was Robert's," Francis said.

Ian turned until the gun was trained on Francis. "Francis Byrde. It's been a few years."

Hugh could see Robin tensing to move and he shook his head at him. It would be too easy for Ian to lose control and begin shooting. That was the last thing they needed.

Think McHughes! Think!

"The treasure," Ian said. "Where is it?"

"It's not here," Francis assured him.

Ian's eyelid twitched and he took a step forward, dragging Robin with him. "You've removed it!" he shouted.

"It was never here," Malik spoke up.

Hugh could hear the coldness of the vampire's voice for the first time. He realised he was trying to use his charm on Ian, but it didn't appear to be having any effect.

"Who are you?" Ian barked out, startled. Hugh realised he hadn't registered Malik and had not been expecting him.

"Who I am is irrelevant," Malik replied. "What treasure do you seek?"

Ian took a step backwards as he eyed them up. Then he stopped stock still and Robin darted from under his arm and ran across to join the others. He was pulled into a rough hug by Malik who whispered something in his ear.

As Hugh watched Ian, he noticed movement behind him. An armed policeman moved out of the shadows, aiming his gun at Swales.

"Give me your weapon," The man barked. Ian jumped and the gun went off.

#

Falcon

Falcon ducked as Ian's weapon discharged. He could hear the police shouting at Ian to get on the ground now! Quickly looking around, he could see that no-one had been hurt when the gun went off. Everyone else had ducked too and were now hauling themselves up off the ground.

DI Matlock entered the room just as the armed police support officer was putting Ian into cuffs and hauling him to his feet.

"Ma'am," the officer acknowledged Matlock.

"Take him down the station, Tate. Thank you for your

assistance today."

The man nodded and began leading Ian away, who was still shouting about the treasure and that he'd get them one day. His noise gradually faded, and they turned to face Matlock and the other police officers.

"You set us up!" Hugh almost shouted at Matlock. "When you came by the bookshop yesterday to let us know we could come back here, you knew then you were laying a trap for him."

Matlock held up her hand at Hugh and stopped him in his tracks. "It was a tactical move. I couldn't be sure Ian would come here, but we caught sight of someone hanging around Ogleforth yesterday who matched Ian's profile. Unfortunately, we were too late to arrest him. It was thought there was a good chance he'd return again when he could. "

"You could have warned us, Deidre." Hugh slumped into one of the chairs and Falcon went over to him to give him his support.

Francis was having a low-voiced conversation with Robin, making sure his youngest son was okay. Robin had been late as he'd had a meeting at his shop that he hadn't been able to put off. It had just been bad luck that he'd turned up at the same time as Swales.

They, along with Malik, came to join Falcon and Hugh near the chairs and faced Matlock and her team.

"What now?" Falcon asked.

"Now we question him and determine his fitness for standing trial. He faces a string of charges from kidnap to murder."

"Deidre." Francis moved forward and shook the DI's hand. "I would say it's good to see you, but perhaps not under these circumstances."

"Francis," she acknowledged. "I really am sorry that I was unable to warn you all."

Falcon watched his father frown at her. He wasn't sure he agreed with her assessment of the situation but knew that she'd done what she thought was right.

"And who is this?" she asked as she turned towards Malik.

"An old friend of mine," Francis said. "Detective Inspector Deidre Matlock, this is Malik Lord. He is visiting York for the first time in a few years. We were discussing the book collection with him, as he has an interest in antiquarian books."

"Pleased to meet you." Matlock shook Malik's hand before stepping back. Malik was looking at her as though she was an oddity. Falcon guessed she was to him. He'd last been up and around in the Victorian era when women had not even been involved in policing, let alone as officers in charge.

"I'll be in touch." Falcon looked over as Matlock spoke to Hugh. "Let me know when you're back in Manchester."

"I'm not going back," Hugh answered, standing up. "Well, only to get my things. I'm moving here to York. The Swales Agency is no more. I'll be working with Francis from now on."

Matlock was surprised, Falcon could see that. She didn't say anything though, just nodded. She left the room followed by the remaining officers who had been with her.

After the police had gone, they didn't stay in the underground rooms for long. Malik, it seemed, had lost his appetite for seeing where he'd been held captive all those years. He'd been interested in the weapon wall, but Falcon could see that he was weary of it all now.

"Time to go home," he said.

Hugh grinned at him. "Home. I like that idea."

Falcon took his hand and they walked with the others out of the tunnels and into the bright sunlight of an early June afternoon. As they headed towards the Minster and away from the underground rooms, Falcon felt as though a weight had been lifted from his shoulders, for the first time since Father McKenzie had visited him. It felt like their place in this story had ended and they needed to move on now with their lives.

They agreed to meet up with Francis and the others for dinner at Francis's house in the countryside. He was going to take Gil there for the last couple of weeks he'd be in plaster. The idea was Gil could work for Francis from the house. Hugh had already texted Imogen to let her know it was safe to come home. He'd got a big thumbs up back from her and a note to say she'd be back in the UK in couple of days.

By the time they got back to the bookshop, it had already closed for the day. Abbie was just in the process of locking the doors and the young plainclothes officer DC Turner was there once more. It looked as though they could become an item. Falcon shook the other man's hand, warned him he better treat his niece well, then led Hugh into the shop and through to his study at the back of the building.

Turning, he pulled the other man into his arms. "Here we are," he said, before leaning in and kissing him. What started out slow and sweet ended up heavy and possessive. Hugh clung to him and pushed him towards the stairs and the bedroom. Going eagerly, Falcon tried to keep kissing him as they made their way up the stairs. Bits of clothing littered the area before they'd even got as far as the bedroom. Before he knew it, he was on his back on the bed and Hugh had taken his entire length down his throat.

He groaned. He'd found out his boyfriend gave great head, and this was no exception.

"Yes!" he ground out and thrust up to meet the other man's mouth. It wasn't long before he came.

Feeling relaxed and sated, he turned to Hugh, who grinned at him. He laid back and pulled Hugh into his arms. They lay there for a moment, coming down from their high, before Falcon rolled over to face Hugh. He stroked the other man's face as he held his breath and stared into his eyes. He really was beautiful.

"You know I love you," he stated.

Hugh grinned. "I do." He pulled Falcon in for a kiss. "I love you too, Fal. I can't imagine my life now without you in it."

"Fortunately, you don't need to." Falcon pulled him back into a bruising kiss and lost himself in the moment.

Finally, it felt as though he was home. It was time for him to live his life, with Hugh by his side. Time for Falcon to fly.

Epilogue

Hugh

"That's the last of it," Hugh said as he stood in his empty flat in Manchester, taking in the views of the hills in the distance, and the canal below him for one final time.

"Are you sad to be leaving?" Falcon asked, coming up and putting his arms around him.

"A bit," Hugh replied, leaning back into his lover's embrace. "It's time though, this part of my life is over."

They had one last quick look around the flat before Hugh locked it up for the last time. It had sold quite quickly, and they were going to drop off the keys to the estate agents on their way out of Manchester. He was sad leaving this place as it had been a great area to live and a good place to be when he'd been employed by Swales's Agency, but it was time to move on. His new life in York with Falcon was where he wanted to put his efforts now.

The removal van they'd hired was packed with his things. Where they were going to put it all he didn't know. The flat above the bookshop he now shared with Falcon wasn't that big. Some of it would fit, the rest would go into storage until he decided what to do with it.

"Dinner at Dad's tonight," Falcon reminded him, and Hugh smiled. He always enjoyed dinner at Francis's place. The siblings sometimes reminded him of squabbling children, but they all loved and looked out for each other.

"How's Robin?" he asked.

It had been six months since they'd awakened Malik the sleeping vampire and Robin had been his almost constant companion whilst he was recovering. He'd taken him out, shown him modern day York, introduced him to new technology and encouraged him to meet with Andrew at Leconfield Hall to compare notes. Then, just over a week ago, Malik said he had to go. He had to check on something and it was urgent. That was it, he was gone. There one minute, gone the next. Robin had wandered around for a couple of days looking as though someone had stolen his favourite toy.

"He says he's okay," Falcon replied. "Said Malik had texted him and apologised for leaving suddenly and that he'd see him soon."

"Does he know why he went?"

"I don't think so. If he does, he's keeping it to himself."

After a quick stop to drop off the keys, Hugh manoeuvered the rented van out onto the motorway and sped up to match the flow of the traffic around them. He hoped Robin was okay. He'd come to like Falcon's little brother, all his brothers really, since meeting them.

Falcon reached across and squeezed his hand, not letting go until Hugh had to change gear. He turned to smiled at his lover, his thoughts going to the ring in his pocket that he and Imogen had picked out a couple of weeks ago. All he needed was to find the right time to ask the man he loved to marry him.

Hugh found he was happy properly for the first time in many years. He could almost shout with joy, but instead, he reached over and joined hands with Falcon again. He was so glad his erstwhile employer had sent him to watch over Falcon Byrde.

Navigating the traffic with ease and familiarity, they made their way back to York and their future life.

Hugh pulled up in Stonegate in the dark December evening. It was cold and beginning to rain, the shops around them were mostly closed, but there were still a some people around, looking for somewhere to eat or get a drink. York's tourists never stopped coming, even in winter.

Falcon's brothers joined them at the truck and began moving things into Fal's shop. Those going into storage stayed in the van, and Hugh would take them to the storage place in the morning.

After saying goodbye to the brothers, he and Falcon entered the flat above the bookshop. It looked a lot less neat than it normally did, but Hugh was glad to have his things around him.

Falcon had headed straight for the kitchen to get dinner under way and Hugh began unpacking boxes that belonged in that room. He stopped to watch Falcon for a while, then grinned.

"Hey," he said, dropping to one knee.

Falcon spun around and gaped when he found him on the floor.

"Hugh?"

"Falcon Byrde." Hugh coughed, the emotion getting to him. "I love you more than anything. Please say you'll marry me?"

Falcon dropped to his knees and grabbed Hugh, pulling

him in tight. "I love you too, baby. It would be my honour to marry you."

Hugh pulled him in until he was straddling his knees, then he was kissing the man he loved with all he had. He pulled away after a few moments and smiled at his fiancé.

"It's going to be a great life," he whispered into Falcon's ear. "I'm so glad I get to spend it with you."

Author's Note

Authors Note

Thank you for reading my latest book. I hope you enjoyed it. Please feel free to leave a review or a rating on Amazon or Goodreads. Reviews really do help indie authors get their books out there.

Leconfield Hall is a fictional stately home in Leconfield, East Yorkshire. It and the characters Andrew, Percy, Walker etc. were featured in my harem duology Lady Emma's Diaries and Legacy in Crystal.

Gilead Summerbell is based on real life Antiquarian Gillyatt Sumner (1793-1875). I changed his age a bit to fit in with my own timeline, but the rest (apart from the spell book) is all Gillyatt.

Stonegate Alley was a real shopping area when I lived in York in the 1980s. It was demolished in the early 2000s and is now either flats or empty ground. The entrance from Stonegate is still there, though locked up.

As far as I know there are no tunnels under the Minster! Wouldn't it be fun if there were?

Acknowledgements

Acknowledgments

I'd like to thank my wonderful editor Claire from C L Jennison Editing. All the members of my writer's group Writer's@... who brighten up my Monday mornings.

My contact details

Website www.carolkerrygreenbooks.com.

I love to hear from my readers, you can contact me at carolkerrygreenbooks@gmail.com

My Facebook group is at https://www.facebook.com/groups/680988973201857/ do come along and join in. I do cover reveals and snippets about my current writing there.

My Newsletter – download a free short story set in my Donati Chronicles universe https://carol-kerry-green-books.ck.page/fbe2d4a251

Also by Carol Kerry-Green

Also by Carol Kerry-Green

The Donati Chronicles

Of Blood & Shadows

Living in Shadows

Out of the Shadows*

The Coterie

Lady Emma's Dairies

Legacy in Crystal

The Byrdes of York

Flight of the Falcon

* * *

Robin in Winter*

Oleader's Path*

*Coming 2025

Printed in Dunstable, United Kingdom

71048069R00157